SINGLE *Sal*

EMMY LOVE

Book design and illustration by Rebecca Rhodes

ISBN 978-0-473-65511-2 (paperback)

ISBN 978-0-473-65512-9 (ebook)

ISBN 978-0-473-65513-6 (kindle)

www.emmylove.com

Give Away!

Get a sneak peek into Sal's life with the TV pilot script that inspired the novel! Download it FREE at emmylove.com where you can also read blog posts about all things love, and be the first to know when *Singled Out*—the sequel to *Single Sal*—is released.

For all the single ladies,
may you find your happily ever after

Contents

Chapter 1

Sal

CALL ME SAL, SINGLE Sal. Well, that's what my friends call me anyway. As much as I love them, lately that nickname has been really frizzing my hair! Like, what's wrong with being single? Then again, who can blame them. Not once in my twenty-nine years have I been in a serious relationship. *Cue the violin.*

Yes, some people pity me because there's never been a long-term man in my life. But I've also never had to deal with bed hogging, farting, washing stinky underwear or justifying where I've been. No pity for me, thanks. I am a-okay!

Sigh. Alright, as much as I adore my space, it does get lonely sometimes. It's not like I'm butt ugly, batshit crazy (actually that's debatable), or even shy. I'm an independent career woman, err ... just without the career. *Hmm.* Maybe I *do* want a relationship. Maybe I'm scared, weird or super selective. Maybe I'm just Single Sal.

The thought of dating strangers freaks me out. Every date I've been on has felt like a job interview to be a cleaner and cook by day and a call girl by night. And just when I'm convinced that a guy is ready to commit, he drops me like a hot tortilla except *I'm* the one who gets burned! After a while rejection takes its toll, and I get enough of that already in showbiz.

You know what? My friend Piper's right. I'm not going to find my soulmate watching reruns of *Dr Love* in my fat pants every night—it's time to swap them for my big girl pants. And that's why I'm going on a date!

I put on my favorite nineties playlist and dance into the bathroom. I flutter my false lashes and tilt my face to check my contouring. Carefully I paint my lips hot pink, the shade of lipstick perfectly matching my cute figure-hugging dress. I run my fingers through my long platinum hair and eyeball myself in the mirror.

"I am girlfriend material."
"I am girlfriend material."
"I am girlfriend material."

The more affirmations I repeat, the more my confidence grows. Who knew words had so much power?—Well, my old therapist did I guess.

I sway my body to the beat.

"This date is going to go really well."
"This date is going to go really well."

Perfectly in time I drop my booty low, thinking I'm Beyonce. *Ooh, mm hm mmm hot, hot.* I'm whipping my hair back and forth when I glimpse my roommate Carlos standing in the living room trying to hold back laughter. I recoil in shock, clasping a hand to my chest. "How long have you been standing there?"

"Wayyy too long!" he drawls with an arrogant laugh.

My mood turns sour. I growl and biff the bathroom door shut. But I can still hear his irritating voice.

"Thanks for making my night, Sal! Oh, and I'm sure your date will go *really well.*"

I scowl at my reflection. *Why is he so annoying!* I'm more determined than ever for my date to go perfectly. I push my modest boobs up and add some flicks to the corners of my eyes with liquid liner. I take a selfie pulling the classic duck face, and send it to my best friends Fran and Piper with the caption:

Wish me luck, ladies. I'm going in!

I glance across the table at my date, Ronnie, as he devours a giant bowl of meatballs. I try not to look at his *Lord of the Rings* T-shirt, but it clashes ridiculously against his camo-print cargo shorts. My eyes sweep the restaurant, full of noisy, happy patrons. Then my gaze turns back to Ronnie. The lighting is so bright that I can't help but notice every wrinkle and age spot on his face.

Listening to him spit out meaningless words while chewing puts me off my tofu salad. Instead, I sip my cosmopolitan and try to act interested.

"I think it's so cool that you're an actress. I mean, who isn't around here? Have you ever worked with Peter Jackson?"

I shake my head and let him continue. "My dream was always to play Frodo in *The Lord of the Rings*. Do you think I could play Frodo?" he asks passionately.

My eyes bounce around the room as I think of a reply. "What about Gollum?"

He stops chewing. I'm afraid I've offended him and cautiously wait for his reply. He starts chewing again. "Oh yeah, I've always wanted to be a character actor. Thanks!"

The sound of my phone trills from my bag and gets louder as I bring it to my ear. Normally I wouldn't answer it on a date, but I'm secretly delighted by the interruption.

"Sorry, Ronnie. I should take this."

He gestures his approval as he shoves another meatball in his mouth.

"Hi Mom, I can't talk right now. I'm in the middle of a date."

"A date!? How wonderful dear. With a boy?"

A fiery whisper escapes my mouth. "No, with a freaking alien, Mom. *Yes, with a boy!*" I hear her exclaim to my dad that I'm not a lesbian. *Like, is she for real!*

I huff. "Mom, are you there?"

"Sorry sweetheart, I'm here. I'll leave you to your date! It was just a quick call to see if you want me to organize something for your thirtieth birthday?"

"Sure, whatever. I better go."

"Okay, darling, have fun and be safe."

I slip my phone back into my bag and smile at Ronnie. "Sorry about that."

My gaze roams over him. I'm hesitant to say what I'm about to say. "Hey, um, Ronnie, you look a lot different than when we met on set."

"Oh darn! I was hoping you wouldn't notice. That knight suit sure did me a favor, ah? I normally wear a toupee but on my way out the door a scary-looking woodpecker took off with it, the cheeky thing. I tried to run after it but I didn't want to get all sweaty for the date, you know."

I laugh hesitantly. "Totally."

"And I had to wear my glasses to get a good look at you." He tilts his glasses, and his eyes bulge when they reach my chest. "Ronnie likes what he sees."

Repulsed by his salivating mouth, I pull up the top of my dress and wish I had worn my sparkly pink turtleneck instead.

"I'm still the same person inside," he claims, laughing.

Did he really just say that? I choke on my drink at the hypocrisy, considering the way he just ogled my body.

"Oh, man—these meatballs are so good. I love meat. I love steak, sausages, and beef stew, but you can't beat a good old meatball in your mouth." He offers me a seductive wink. I fight back the urge to throw up all over his meatballs. Talking with a mouth full of food and eating noisily are pet peeves I cannot compromise on. Not even for Henry Cavill.

"Are you all right over there?" he asks.

I force a smile and feel my face distort into a manic grimace. But at this point the more unappealing I look, the better.

"You sure look sexy when you pull that face," he says, glancing at my untouched salad. "Saving room for dessert, I see?"

"I've lost my appetite."

"What's *your* favorite meat then?"

"I'm a vegetarian."

Ronnie swallows his mouthful, puts his knife and fork down, and leans back in his chair. *"Game CHANGER!"*

"Meat doesn't agree with me, if you know what I mean." I pinch my nose with one hand and flap the other in front of my face.

"Ooo—nasty!"

"Yep. It goes straight through me. It's enough to put any man off!"

He leans across the table toward me, getting so close that I reflexively cringe away. "I'll have you know I *like* a little nasty."

Slowly I reach for my handbag, as Ronnie sits back. He snaps his fingers. "I've got it!"

I freeze.

"I can cook two separate meals! Well, when I say *me*, I mean my mom. She's good like that. She'll even make our bed and do our laundry if you behave."

His creepy wink inspires me to snatch up my phone and start a fake conversation.

"*Mom!* I told you I'm on a date!" My face drastically changes as I put my acting chops to the test. "Oh no, not again? Okay, I'll be there right away."

I stand up and sling my bag over my shoulder. "I'm sorry, I have to go."

"What's wrong?"

"I need to pick up my kids from my mom's place. One of them got stuck in the cat flap again. I keep telling little Junior he's not a cat. Kids, huh!"

"You didn't mention you had kids?"

"Normally I don't bring them up until the third date. Having five kids seems to turn men off. But the cat's out of the bag now! *Me-ow.*" I nervously laugh and make halfhearted claw gestures with my hands.

Ronnie peers down at his last meatball, then looks back at me with crybaby eyes. Guilt creeps in, so I throw a twenty-dollar bill onto the table. "Okay—bye!"

He stands up, and I can feel him watch me strut my way out of the restaurant. "Sally! I'll call you!"

Chapter 2

Sal

"I have margaritas!" Fran squeals, handing them out to Piper and me as we lounge in a booth, soaking up the lively Friday night atmosphere at our favorite bar, Tequila Tavern.

"Francesca!" Before the glass touches Fran's mouth, she lowers it reluctantly.

"Yes, Sal?"

"That's not a real margarita, is it?"

"No, but can I please pretend for one night that it is?"

"Six months will go by fast, Fran. You've got this," Piper says, twirling her pink cocktail umbrella between her long pastel-tinted nails.

"Don't remind me," Fran grumbles.

"Since when did our margaritas come with these cute little umbrellas and with lime *and* cherries?!" Piper pops the cherry in her mouth and licks her red lips. "Yum!"

"I asked Betty to make them extra special. It's not every day Sal books a job!" Fran raises her glass. "Cheers, bitches!"

Piper's head swings around to me. I can see she's confused that I didn't tell her. I dart an eye roll at Fran.

"What? It's great news."

Piper looks expectantly at me. I offer her a small smile. "It's just a silly commercial, Piper. Honestly, no big deal."

"That's incredible, Sal! These things can lead to a big break. What's the commercial for?"

Great. Here we go. I fumble around awkwardly before answering in my teeniest voice. "Condoms."

Fran puts her hand to her ear. "Speak up, girlfriend. I thought you said condoms?"

"No, Fran, I think she said *pom-poms*," Piper suggests.

I huff out a sigh. There's no escaping this convo. "No, Piper. Condoms!"

I recoil at the sight of Fran spitting out her drink, which her lime green shirt catches the majority of. The volume of my voice was louder than I expected, going by the emerging stares and laughter of a group of hipsters at a nearby table. I squeeze my eyes shut and compose myself.

"You left that part out, you sneaky minx!" Fran says, dissolving in giggles.

"And now you know why."

"Do you even know what one looks like?" Fran teases, twirling her curly black hair around her fingers.

Fran was always bold and said what she thought. People either love or hate her. But *I* love her. We've been friends since high school, and even though she can be a pain in my ass, she tells me what I need to hear.

"Do *you?*" I enquire, smiling brightly, pursing my lips.

"Sweetheart, if you're insinuating that I need to use condoms more often, then you would be correct!"

Piper and I giggle. Fran puts her hands on her belly. "This will be my third and last child. Eating a packet of Oreos gives me more pleasure than sex right now. But you, Sal, are still single *without* the mingle."

"I tried mingling at that tedious speed dating thing. And, guys! You still haven't asked how my date went last night! What kind of besties are you?"

"Yes, of course hon! You didn't say who with?" Piper asks enthusiastically.

"Ugh! This random guy I met on set at the commercial. But he seemed a little too keen."

"Sounds better than the arrogant douchebags you usually date," Fran says.

I sigh, staring out the window at all the disgustingly happy couples walking by. "I've already made peace with being Single Sal, the lonely dog lady, for the rest of my life." I shift my focus back to Fran and speak with conviction. "What's important right now is my career."

I notice Piper looking at Fran and I know they're probably thinking, *What career?*

Piper turns her Instagram-worthy face to me and smiles. "What happened to that hot dad you were crushing on?"

"Ugh—Zac Johnston. He hasn't messaged me since I slept with him over a month ago. I don't know what I was thinking. He invited me over for a late dinner, but all he had to offer was beer, crisps and a Bruce Willis movie."

"What a dick! Aw man, sounds like you got played, girl," Fran says, shaking her head.

"Oh, honey. You poor thing," Piper adds sympathetically.

"It was my fault. I just thought it would grow into something more. But now I see him every day when he drops Annabelle off at class, and he pretends he doesn't even know me! It's so awkward."

I look to Piper for comfort. As much as I rely on Fran to tell me the truth, I rely on Piper to tell me the lie. I'm not saying she's a liar. She just has a soothing way about her that always makes me think everything will be okay—even if it clearly won't! She's like a magical unicorn with *the best* taste in shoes.

"I don't get it. He would always send snaps saying how much he missed me. And now—poof!"

"Sal, if a grown man is snapchatting you instead of texting or calling as a decent human would do, that is a *huge* red flag. I'm sorry, but Fran called it. You got played."

Okay, that wasn't the response I expected from Piper. But she's right. How could I have been so naive? *Come on, Sal! This wasn't your first rodeo!*

"What are you doing sleeping with dads, anyway? Isn't that, like, forbidden if you're a teacher?" Fran asks.

"He was charming and alluring. When he walked into class, I never knew if he wanted to kill me or kiss me. I liked the thrill. I liked the distraction."

"Distraction from?" Fran asks casually before plonking a tortilla chip in her mouth.

"If you hadn't noticed, I'm nearly thirty without a boyfriend. I have a student loan I can't pay off, I live with a guy who hates me, and a condom commercial has been the high-light of my life lately! At least you have Jamal, the twins, and another baby to love." My eyes bounce to Piper. "And Piper! Who can compete with you? You're senior editor of *Brides and Beauty*, and you look like a Victoria's Secret model."

Piper smooths her forest-green pantsuit with her hands and flicks her long chestnut locks to the side. "Come on, Sal. You've accomplished lots with your life."

"Yeah, you were on *Sex in the Suburbs*. You were amazing!" Fran says with bright eyes.

"Except they killed my character, and I haven't heard from my agent since. I'm so over being typecast as the blonde bimbo. Heck! I couldn't even get an audition for *Barbie*."

"It takes an intelligent actress to pull off a blonde bimbo. Margot Robbie in *Barbie* is a perfect example," Piper counters.

Fran snorts, "Barbie isn't a bimbo." She turns to me with one of her high-and-mighty looks, and I can tell I'm in for a right old treat.

"Maybe you need to consider ditching the six-inch heels and low-cut bodycon dresses. Get rid of those hair extensions, cover up a little, and wear less eye makeup so we can see how beautiful your eyes truly are, *then* you'll have a better chance of playing respectable characters."

"Fran! This is what the studio wanted! I have a cult following because of this look."

"Sal! Most of that *following* are just men who want to sharpen their blunt-ass pencils!"

"Huh?" I ask, cute memories of me in my classroom sharpening pencils flood my brain. I must say, I *am* pretty good at sharpening pencils.

"Get *laid* Sal! They want to bow-chicka-wow-wow, they wanna pound your p—"

"Stop Fran! I think she gets it!" Piper cuts in, and I'm thankful for her prudish ways.

Fran continues, "No wonder you haven't found the right guy yet. I'm telling ya, you're baiting the wrong men *and* roles with this look. I'm sorry girl, but it's time I finally said something."

"I thought you loved my Barbie-meets-Dolly-Parton inspired look? Hello, they're icons for a reason."

"I did! But in the last year it seems Barbie lost her way and got a job at the strip club."

"Fran!" exclaims Piper.

I gasp, rising from my seat. Before I can defend myself, Fran bursts into tears apologizing for her frisky hormones. I take a moment before I sit back down.

"Settle down Fran, we're fine." She smiles at me through her tears, and my eyes seek comfort from Piper. But all I get back is a sorrowful smile that tells me she feels the same way.

"Sal, I used to love how you projected your personality through your colorful clothes. But I think Fran's trying to say that since you changed your style to please the studio, we've noticed you don't seem happy. You don't even like dating."

I try not to show I agree with her because the truth hurts too much. Ever since I sold myself to a studio that replaced me with the next best thing, I guess I haven't been myself. Now I'm holding on to the image they wanted me to portray, and I don't even know who I'm doing it for. I *know* I have the skills to play more serious roles. Somehow, I will prove it to everyone. As for men?

"What if they get to know me, see me without makeup, and then run?"

Piper's eyes wash over Fran before they land on me. "Who wouldn't want to be with a fun and kind person like you? You're not the typical girl next door, but LA has enough of them already. There *is* a human to love under all that glam, you know."

I laugh, but deep down, the thought of wearing no makeup makes me want to isolate myself in the wilderness among the animals like Snow White. *Ain't no one seeing this face without makeup.*

"I applaud your commitment to acting, but at the cost of missing out on true love? I don't know anyone who's stayed single for as long as you have," Piper says.

Fran puts her finger to her mouth. "Asexual people!"

Piper rolls her eyes at Fran. "No. They have relationships, just without the sex."

Fran continues, "Mormons? Monks? Amish? Ooh, I've got it! Priests!" She shakes her head. "Actually, nah—they're the worst."

"Are you seriously comparing me to monks and priests? Do I look like a priest to you?"

Fran smiles, and my heart sinks, visualizing being old and crippled without a career to show for myself and with no one to love. I feel Piper rest her hand on my shoulder, which snaps me out of my pathetic pity party.

"We just want to see you happy, Sal. Aren't you tired of being a cameo in these men's lives? Because I'm tired of seeing you get hurt."

I nod in agreement.

Piper continues. "Don't you deserve better?"

I nod again.

Piper slaps her dainty hand on the table. "Say it, Sal!"

"I deserve better."

"Isn't it time for you to be the leading lady for once? Don't you want to meet your own Ken?!"

Her passion is contagious, and I shoot to my feet like I've been given orders by a sergeant. "Yes, I do!"

The enthusiasm in my voice carries through the bar, catching the attention of the nearby hipsters. I nervously laugh, sitting back down. Then I lean into the table and lower my voice.

"So—what do I do now?"

Fran clasps her hands together. "Simple, start wearing clothes *you* like, not what you think the studio or men want you to wear. Start dating guys who remember when your birthday is. Guys that will give you flowers, not STDs or a cheap Netflix and chill date."

I twist my lips to one side, realizing the only flowers I've ever received were from my parents at my drama school graduation nine years ago. "Flowers, huh?"

Piper twinkles an eyebrow and nods with conviction. "Flowers, honey."

"It does sound nice. I did always think I'd be settled down by thirty."

"What do you have, like five weeks?" Fran asks, smiling.

"Four," I reply, watching her face fade into a dubious look.

"My parents married within six weeks. What do you have to lose?" Piper says in her perky voice.

I refrain from bringing up Piper's parents' ugly divorce and watch them as they eyeball me intensely. I break. "Fine, you're right! I do deserve love. How hard can it be, right? People fall in love every day, so why can't it be me?"

"Atta girl!" Fran cries, clapping her hands.

We salute with our glasses. Piper signals in the direction of a seedy-looking man staring at us from the corner of the bar.

She lowers her voice, "What about the guy at three o'clock, Sal?"

I catch a peek of the man leering at me drunkenly. "Eww!"

Finally, I pull my bright yellow Volkswagen convertible into my Glendale apartment parking lot.

I take my bag from the passenger seat, lock the car, and make my way up the old, crooked stairs that lead to my humble apartment on the third floor. Every time I take the elevator, I remind myself that I save money on a gym membership by taking the stairs. But it does help that the elevator is always out of order.

Carlos, my terrifically annoying roommate—make-up artist to … not exactly *stars*, but people whom I concede *are* star-adjacent—is probably home by now. *Fabulous.*

Counting my last steps, I'm relieved to be at the front door. Then I open it to find Carlos in a position no one would want to see on their kitchen table.

"Oh my god, *gross!*" I gasp, horrified.

Carlos screams and pulls away from his boyfriend, Danny, who looks just as shocked as me.

"Can you at least knock, Sal?!"

"But I live here!" I crouch down to pick up the love of my life, a brown and white chihuahua named Oscar.

"Oscar will be traumatized now!" I walk back out and slam the front door while I control my panting breaths. "Are you okay, my baby boy?" I coo while Oscar licks my face.

Moments later, Danny rushes through the door in a flutter and disappears down the hallway. Before the door shuts, I barge through like a bull and see Carlos trying to put his baby-pink mesh-panel leggings back on.

Carlos is gorgeous. His Mom is originally from Mexico and they both have soft brown skin and shiny dark hair. But right now I do not want to see those long pretty legs, especially not naked in my kitchen! *Like hello!*

With narrow eyes, I stare at his face instead. "Are you wearing my candy-floss lipstick?"

"No!"

I take a step closer. "Yes, you are!"

"No, I'm not!" he snaps defensively as his face flushes red. He scurries to his room, trying not to trip over himself while still pulling his leggings up. "Go away!" he howls before his bedroom door bangs shut.

"What is your *problem?*" I demand passionately.

I huff, and glance in revulsion at the kitchen. Then I look down at Oscar curled around my feet. "Hungry bebe?"

Oscar yelps a little bark.

"Me neither." I swoop him up and make my way into the living room. I kick off my heels, dump my bag, and settle into my pink fluffy couch cushions.

I turn on the TV and a Maxwell's Meat commercial blasts through the screen. The commercial ends with a catchy tune and an older man and his wife chanting the slogan, *"Feel good about what you eat with Maxwell's Meat, the meat you can't beat."*

"Ugh—yuck," I mutter, switching it off. I look into Oscar's big brown eyes. "I think it's time I find you a daddy."

Chapter 3

Sal

WARM ORANGE LIGHT SHINES through the trailing leaves of a willow tree growing atop a gentle hill, highlighting my white summer dress. I run my fingers through the hair of a ruggedly striking man with olive skin and whiskey-brown eyes, who's nestled in my lap. I whisper into his ear then run down the hill, giggling like a teenager.

"You'll never catch me, Zac, never!"

Zac lopes after me like a lazy lion after its prey. Just before he catches me, a flock of roosters appear and surround us. Deafening crowing noises grow louder and louder until we fall to our knees in terror—the roosters peck at our bodies before pecking at my face. I cover my ears and let out a petrified scream.

"Ahhhhhhh!" I spring into an upright position with my hands covering my ears. Loud echoes of my rooster alarm penetrate the room. I'm relieved Oscar's still asleep as I lean over to my bedside table and jab at my phone to silence it. As soon as I see five missed calls from Ronnie, I throw the phone across the room and snuggle into Oscar. Then the inertia of sleep clears

and a little gasp catches in my throat. *"Wait, what day is it, Oscar?"*

I bounce out of bed, searching through the mountain of clothes on the floor that I still haven't sorted since getting ready for my disastrous date. After finding my phone under a tanning mitt, I check the time. Eight thirty-five am. *Shit!* Usually I'd be up before eight to beat the traffic and get to my nine o'clock drama class, which I teach every morning at a local elementary school. With no time for a shower, I throw on a yellow daisy-print shirt, a denim skirt and the first pair of shoes I find, strappy white wedges.

After falling over while running to the bathroom, I quickly brush my teeth, tie my hair in a top bun and run to the kitchen to get my car keys. On the counter there's a note from Carlos:

<u>*Don't eat my bread!*</u>

Whenever he underlines his silly little notes, I know he's angry. *Honestly, it was one slice. What a loser!* I quickly fill Oscar's bowl with canned food and run to the elevator, which is *still* out of order.

Hoping no one sees me clomp my way down the stairs like a constipated hyena, I finally make it to my car and join the heavy morning traffic. Listening to empowering affirmations, which I drown out by chiming in loudly, calms me.

The ocean of cars grind to a halt. Although I'm annoyed, I gladly use the time to flip down the car mirror and put my hair in a side ponytail and apply some pink lipstick. I pump a few sprays of Britney's *Believe* and flash a quick pout at my reflection. The traffic starts moving again. With five minutes left until nine, I feel I can just make it.

I drive to my usual spot, but it's taken by another car. *What the heck!* This can't be happening. My eyes catch the time on the dashboard. Five past nine. *Fuck!* With no parking anywhere in the area, I'm forced to drive a block away, where I snag a free spot before dashing back toward the elementary school.

The top half of my body wilts over as I rest my hands on my knees. I catch my breath and approach the sliding doors to the school's foyer. Then I see Angela, a young teacher with purple hair carrying what looks like a box of personal belongings, who storms through the doors with so much force she collides into me.

"Watch it!" she snaps.

"I'm sorry, Angela. I thought you saw me coming."

Angela continues walking.

"Angela! Are you okay?"

She looks back at me like she has something to say, but after a second, carries on.

"Weird," I mutter.

I rush past Jane, the receptionist, who glances up at me from behind her desk, "Ah, Sal!"

"Morning Jane! Sorry, I'm running late—talk to you after class!"

I turn the corner to the corridor and abruptly bump into the playboy himself, Zac Johnston.

"Someone looks like they're in a hurry," Zac says in his deep, controlled tone.

Flustered by his presence, I step back and toy with my side pony. "Zac! How are you?"

He smirks. "Sorry I haven't been in touch after—well, you know. It's just that I've been busy with Annabelle and all."

I try my hardest to act like I don't care, even though I cried for days after he ignored my messages. "Don't sweat it!"

His intoxicating eyes make me forget I'm even late. I watch him scratch his ear before he glances back toward my classroom. "I didn't think you'd be here today?"

"Oh?" I say curiously.

"Yeah, another teacher is taking your class."

"What?!" I brush past him and peer through the classroom window to discover he's telling the truth. As I grasp the door handle with my sweaty hand, about to burst in, I hear the stern voice of Mr. Jeffries, the school principal.

"Miss Gardner."

I turn, and there he is with his giant nose, violating my personal space.

"Mr. Jeffries! I'm so sorry I'm late."

"Can I have a word?" he asks, raising a flinty eyebrow.

I nod and look around to see Zac, but he's gone. Probably for the best, because as I follow Mr. Jeffries down the corridor, intuition tells me this can't be good.

"Take a seat," Mr. Jeffries says, pushing his office door shut.

I sit on the edge of the chair with my spine so straight I feel like it could snap in half.

"It'll never happen again, Mr. Jeffries. That Monday morning traffic is *not* fun, let me tell you!"

The exacting way he walks around his varnished wooden desk and sits down in his black leather chair gives me an uneasy feeling. For some reason he always smells like marmalade, and reminds me of when I volunteered at the old folk's home where I had to spread it on a million pieces of toast. To lighten the mood, I point at a framed photograph that shows a young woman—probably his daughter—in a graduation robe.

"You must be proud?"

"Oh, I am. She graduated with honors."

"Wow. Where is she now?"

"Chicago. She got an offer she couldn't refuse, and now she's one of the top brain surgeons at St Joseph's Hospital."

"Doctor, ah. Fancy. I wish I went down that path. I hear they get paid a lot more." I nervously laugh, knowing I can't distract him forever.

His demeanor softens as he lets out a small sigh. "Sally, this isn't the first time you've been late. And quite frankly, what you wear to class is inappropriate."

"Oh," I say softly.

"But something else has come to my attention."

I flick my ponytail and brace myself for what's to come.

"Does a parent by the name of Zac Johnston ring any bells?"

As soon as I hear his name, I feel the blood rush to my face and my body shrinks into my chair. "It was just a regretful one-night stand, sir. I'm not even seeing him anymore!"

"That's enough information, Sally. I don't care if it was one night, one month, or one kiss. You know the rules. This could jeopardize our reputation."

I place my hands on either side of the chair and tighten my grip. He must think I'm a total tart. But in truth, except for Zac I haven't had a one-night stand since I was twenty-three—purely because they make me feel like trash the next day. "It'll never happen again, sir."

Mr. Jeffries clears his throat. "No, I'm afraid it won't, because I'm going to have to let you go."

And just like that, five years of loyalty to the longest job I have ever held are gone. I knew this day would come. Who am I, teaching six-year-olds to be confident through acting when I'm just faking confidence myself?

I'm not about to give up that easily though, I have to pay my rent somehow.

"What! No! Please, I need this job. I love the kids—"

"And the kids love you, but you should have thought about that before fooling around with one of our dads. Besides, I've had to fire Miss Rogers, so it's only right for me to let you go also."

"Wait, what? Angela? What did she do wrong?"

He smiles before scrunching up his lips like I should know the answer.

"No! Not with Zac?"

He leans back into his chair, crosses his arms, and looks at me with all-knowing eyes.

"Are you sure?"

"Social media doesn't lie, Sally. And where you're concerned—well, you shouldn't have bragged about it to your colleagues."

"That bastard!"

"Sorry, Sally. Please pack up your locker and leave the premises immediately."

Devastated and dismissed, I gather my things and walk through the foyer with a box containing five-years worth of handmade gifts from kids, lipsticks, and accumulated coffee mugs.

"I'm sorry, dear. I was going to warn you," Jane says compassionately.

"Thanks, Jane. I'll miss this place."

I feel the warm air heating up as I slowly make my way along the street with my head down, regretting ever meeting Zac Johnston. *Social media doesn't lie! Hah!* I kick at an empty Pepsi can on the sidewalk. "I *hate* men!" I lose my balance and fall flat on my backside, the box sliding out of my grasp.

Not knowing whether to scream or cry, I let out a grunt. My watering eyes look up through the hazy, muggy air and I notice a tow truck in the distance hooking up my car. *What the heck!* I get up off the ground and run as fast as my strappy shoes will allow, leaving my spilled box of crap behind.

"*Stop!* That's my car!" I reach the driver just as he starts up his truck. "What are you doing with my car?!" I call frantically, knocking on his window.

He winds the window down. "Ma'am, you were parked in a tow-away zone."

"No, I wasn't!"

Unamused, he points to a 'Tow Away Zone' sign right next to where I was parked.

"Shit!" I look at him, batting my lashes. "Can't you just turn a blind eye for once?"

"Sorry, rules are rules. Plus, I got a quota to reach." He gives me a card. "This is where your car will be going."

"How much will it cost?"

"Anywhere from one hundred twenty-five dollars. But don't expect to get it back anytime soon. Good luck." He switches his blinker on.

My eyes take a second look at the address and realize he's going to drive near my talent agency. I knock on his window again. "Wait!"

"Yes?" his tone is weary.

"Can I catch a ride?"

"No, ma'am. That's against company policy."

"Screw your company policy. You've just taken my car!" I clutch my hands together under my chin and pout my lower lip. "Please, sir. I have no other option. It's so hot, *please*."

His eyes dart to a small photo of himself and a teenage girl stuck to the rearview mirror. He pauses and shakes his head before leaning across to open the passenger door.

"Thank you so much!" I run around the front of the truck and climb in.

"No girl should be walking the streets of LA by herself, even if it *is* only ten in the morning. Where do you need to go?"

Chapter 4

Sal

B*EEP BEEP!* I WAVE goodbye to the truck driver from where I stand on the corner of Melrose Ave in West Hollywood. I walk through the bustle of high-end retail stores, singing buskers, and happy shoppers. There is only one place I need to go, and as soon as I see the giant lettering on top of a glass high-rise announcing *Veronica's Talent Agency*, I know everything will be okay.

My heartbeat thunders faster the closer I get. It's been over a year since I have seen Veronica, which isn't a sign of a flourishing acting career. But if I am out of sight, I am out of mind, and there's only one way to get the attention I need. I turn my phone camera to selfie mode and touch up my lipstick. I flatten my frizzy hair and put on my confident face in the hope that it's enough to mask my inner desperation.

The large glass doors slide open automatically, welcoming me in. Cool air brushes against my sweaty skin as I make my way to the elevator.

Soothing elevator music helps put my mind at ease, then the doors ping open, and a crisp lemon fragrance greets me. The extravagant reception area is full of colorful trailing plants that stand out against the black and white decor.

Observing the larger-than-life portraits of B-list celebrities mounted on the walls, I am reminded of my dream of being up there myself. I remember when I was twenty-one, full of hope and optimism. I had just signed on with Veronica, who promised me great success. However, the roles I got were always supporting characters, in a play if I was lucky. Most of my film roles were the goofy blonde sidekick or the sexy siren that no one took seriously.

At the reception desk, I take a mint from the crystal bowl and pop it in my mouth. "Mm, so good."

I look at the strikingly beautiful receptionist rocking a high bun. She stares back at me with cold curiosity.

"Sorry, I'm so hungry," I say, reaching for another mint. The receptionist clears her throat in a high-pitched manner, and I withdraw my hand.

"Do you have an appointment ..."

"Oh, sorry. You must be new here. I haven't seen you before. Sally Gardner's my name. And no, I don't, but I'm on Veronica's books!"

She flashes me a condescending smile. "Well, then you'll know she sees clients by appointment only."

"Yes, I do know, but it's rather urgent." My eyes rest on the waiting area. "It's okay. I'll wait until she's free."

"Sorry, no appointment, no access. I can make you one?" Her eyes scroll the computer screen in front of her. "Veronica can see you in three weeks. There's a morning appointment on a Tuesday if you'd like it?"

"Three weeks! Please, it'll only take a minute." I walk to the waiting area and catch a glimpse of Veronica stalking around in her glass-walled office, on a phone call. Hesitantly, I sit next to a long-legged blonde who gives me bad vibes. I look up, the receptionist stands in front of me with both hands on her hips.

"I won't disturb anyone, I promise!" I whisper.

"Fine, but you'll be waiting all day," she says, stalking back to her desk.

"Lucky I have all day then." My fake laugh fades as I catch the blonde woman looking at me with superiority.

Subtly, I lean my nose into my armpit and jolt back into my chair in disgust. I only have a few minutes to contemplate life and recite confidence affirmations in my head before Veronica flings her door open with panache. Immediately, I put my best smile on, and so does the blonde woman next to me.

"Monica *dah-ling!*" The blonde woman rises from her chair and receives a kiss on each cheek from Veronica. I observe as they make small talk and tell each other how fabulous they look. I feel invisible. Envy starts to flood my veins. I am not a jealous person, which I am thankful for, but one thing I yearn for is to feel worthy of such compliments. The longer I watch them laugh together, the faster my smile travels south.

Maybe the receptionist is right? I could be waiting all day. My hand shoots out and 'accidentally' tips over a glass of water that's on the low table in front of me.

"Ah—oops!"

Veronica's head spins around just as she's entering her office and she notices me. "Sally! Is that you?"

The receptionist rushes back in. "I'm so sorry, Veronica. She wouldn't leave."

"No need to get your panties in a twist, Lisa. I needed to see her anyway." She smiles at Monica. "Monica, I won't be long. Sally, come on through. Oh, and Lisa, clean this mess up, will you?"

"Of course, Veronica." Lisa swishes out of the waiting room, giving me a contemptuous look as she passes.

My hopeful smile lights up the room as Monica returns to her seat, resentment marring her pretty face.

"Sally! It's been a while, babes," Veronica says, gesturing at me to take a seat. "What brings you here on this fine day?"

I place my hands in my lap and put on a sweet yet professional voice. "Well, I guess it's been a long time since I've booked a job with you. I was wondering if any auditions are coming up?"

"I see. Let me check." Veronica sits down on her transparent acrylic chair and glances fleetingly at her laptop before she replies. "Nope, no auditions, Sally. Well, not for your particular look anyway."

I study the floor to hide my disappointment. What does she mean by my particular look? "Oh, okay," I say.

"But I see you *have* been working, and the job certainly wasn't through me!" Veronica turns the laptop and I'm captivated by her hands, which are stacked with chunky gold rings that dazzle in contrast to her long black nails. "Can you see, Sally?"

I nod, in suspense at what I'm about to view.

"Fabulous," Veronica taps the space bar, and an unflattering close-up of me appears on the screen.

"All I want is—"

"Stop!" I say, reaching out my hands.

Veronica snaps her laptop shut. "Aw, it was just getting good, too."

"Please don't watch it."

"I wish I hadn't."

"I don't know what to say. I thought it would look better than that."

"You're lucky it was so gauche it only aired on YouTube." She picks up a fidget spinner and swirls it effortlessly in a series of loops. "Not bad numbers, considering. It's been live for twelve hours, and it's already had over one hundred thousand views." She leans across her desk and lowers her voice. "My advice though, if you want to avoid the Prozac, *don't read the comments.*"

"I was desperate. It's been so long since I've had an audition, I saw an opportunity and I just thought—"

"Just thought what? A *condom* commercial would look good on your resume? You thought an A-list celebrity like Ryan Gosling would love a leading lady who promotes cheap prophylactics? If you haven't caught on, Sal, this industry is all about image." She looks me up and down, clicking her fingers in my face. "I mean, what is this?"

"I'm having a bad day," I reply shakily.

"Sally, if you can't sell yourself, how do you expect me to? If Dolly Parton and Elton John had a baby—you'd be it." She throws her mane of Cruella hair back and laughs wildly.

I pick my bag up from the floor with trembling hands and place it on my lap. I think about how freaking great it would be if I were the daughter of Dolly Parton and Elton John.

"I normally have myself together. Besides, I thought you said my look was my unique selling point. That I was different?"

"That was a year ago, Sal! Get with the times. I mean, you must be nearly—"

"Thirty." I say softly.

"You'll be mutton in a lamb's world soon, darling. This is Hollywood, not Vegas where all the has-beens go to salvage their last minute of fame. If you haven't made it by now, you'll never make it."

"Please, I just need one audition. I know I have what it takes to play a serious role."

"It's too late, Sal. I'm not representing you anymore."

I clutch onto my bag to save myself from erupting out of my chair. "Please, Veronica! I'll dye my hair. I'll get Botox!"

"And some new clothes?"

"Yes!"

"And take a shower?!"

"Uh-huh!"

Veronica extends her hand in the air and bounces it back. "Ah—no. The queen has spoken."

"Please!" I implore, standing up and toppling my bag to the floor along with my squashed heart.

Veronica leads me to the door without a shred of compassion. "I'm sure you'll find your plan B, Sal, but acting is *not* for you."

"I've never had a plan B!" I clutch my hands together, and my lip starts to wobble. "Please, don't make me beg."

"Alright, time to go. Begging does *not* look good on you." She opens her office door and her attention bounces away from me. "Monica, come on in!"

Monica wears a smug look on her face as she brushes her busty chest past me, where I stand frozen in the middle of the doorway. Veronica tries to close the door, but I won't budge.

"Uh, Sally, do you mind?"

Grudgingly I move aside. I let out a wild huff through flaring nostrils as the door closes. As if deliberately fanning the flames of my humiliation I can hear Veronica and Monica through the glass.

"Congratulations, Monica, you booked fashion week!"

Monica's irritating squeals of excitement make me shudder. A heavy rage floods me as I stomp through the reception area.

I grab the bowl of mints from the desk and tip them into my bag.

"What are you doing, you crazy woman?!" Lisa cries. But I give her a look that makes her step back.

"Okay, you can take them. Please don't hurt me."

I storm toward the elevator, blinking back my tears so I can see which button to press. The doors finally close, and I thump my back against the metal wall and take long deep breaths through my nose. A group of cackling women enter, gushing over their friend's engagement ring. I suppress my emotions and think about what a fool I am for *ever* believing I could be a successful actress and an even bigger fool for prioritizing my dreams over love. As soon as the elevator doors open, I rush outside as if my life depends on it. I fall to my knees and let out an ugly blubbering cry that attracts the concern of nearby pedestrians.

"Are you okay, Miss?" an older man asks worriedly.

"Don't look at me!" I glare around at the growing crowd hovering over me, and I feel ashamed of the person I have become. "Nobody look at me!"

Chapter 5

Sal

SMELLS OF ROASTING COFFEE beans and freshly baked muffins linger around me as I listen to the cafe's mellow music, which blends with the chatter of customers and of staff calling out orders.

Fran sits across from me, practically inhaling an iced chocolate while watching my condom catastrophe on her phone.

"*Woo-wee!* Girl, have you seen how many views this has?"

I take my eyes off the newspaper and fix her with a stern look.

Fran's four-year-old twin boys, Niko and Andre, grab for her phone. "Mama, we watch?"

Fran raises the phone out of reach. "Uh-uh, boys, you're not seeing this. Drink your apple juice, please."

"Ooh—how many views does it have?" Piper asks.

"Nearly a million! You are officially famous, Sal!" Fran's eyes are wide.

"Enough, Fran," I say with no life in my voice.

"If it makes you feel any better, I thought the commercial was very—" Fran pauses before continuing. "Entertaining. Yes, entertaining!"

"Did you read the comments saying I'm the worst actress in the world!? Or that I look like Dr. Evil's twin sister?"

Fran zips her mouth shut, and I shake my head before returning my gaze to the newspaper. My eyes scroll up and down as I cross potential jobs off the list. The one position I haven't obliterated with marker pen is a checkout role at Happy Day Groceries. I entertain the idea for a moment since it's the only local job I know I have a chance at. But the thought of being seen as a checkout girl triggers my anxiety.

I sigh, putting the newspaper down. I dig my fork into my chocolate brownie repeatedly, in a daze.

"So, no luck then?" Piper asks, taking a bite of blueberry muffin.

Aimlessly, I shake my head. "I don't know how much more rejection I can take. It's been two weeks! I mean, how hard is it to find a job around here? I'm already behind on rent. If I don't find some money soon, I'll have to move back in with my parents." I raise an eyebrow. "Which wouldn't be a bad thing, my roommate is driving me insane!"

Piper rolls her eyes. "I'm so glad I don't have to rent anymore. The thought of sharing a bathroom with someone does not sound fun."

"Well, how about sharing lipstick? I'm sure he wears my lipstick when I'm not home."

"That's ... different," Piper allows.

"Right?!" I reply.

Fran speaks up. "Seriously, girl, Jamal and I are happy to lend you some money until you get back on your feet."

"And I've already put the word out to *Brides and Beauty* staff to tell me first if any jobs open up."

"Thanks, guys, I appreciate it. But I'm a grown woman, it's about time I started acting like one. I can do this on my own. You'll see."

Andre and Niko tug at Fran's low-cut floral blouse. "Mama, Mama, how come Aunty Sal has brownie, and we not?"

"No way, boys! Mama needs some peace and quiet today." Fran whispers across the table, "Chocolate turns them into monsters."

I smile, picking up my dairy-free chai latte. The warmth of the mug soothes my worry. Just as I take a sip, my phone buzzes on the wooden table. I glance at the screen. "Ugh!" I shove the phone behind me and ignore it.

"Who is it?!" Fran asks.

"Who do you think?" I reply with dread.

"Gosh, is Ronnie still calling you? He must really like you," Piper says.

"I don't know why. I told him I had five kids! I should have told him I have herpes."

"Eww, Sal. Stay classy. Aw, poor Ronnie," Piper says.

"*Poor Ronnie?* Poor me! I'll *never* get over seeing him eat meatballs like that. *Never!*"

"Don't let one bad date make you give up, Sal," Fran says before shoving her last bite of hotdog in her mouth.

"Okay, tell me, who's going to want to date an unemployed, nearly homeless person with no direction in life at the age of thirty?"

Blank looks cross their faces.

"And please don't say 'Ronnie.' Even he thought I was a famous actress."

Fran waves her phone around. "Uh, you are!"

Piper puts her hand over mine. "Your person is out there, they will love you for who you are—not what you have."

I laugh bitterly. "Vomitsville! Did you get that quote from Facebook? It's shit like that that gives people false hope. This whole 'love me for who I am, not what I have' *BS* only exists in movies like *Titanic*. And look how that turned out! Besides, I don't have time to find love anymore. I have a plan B to work on. *Whatever that is.*"

Piper gets up from her chair, looking radiant in her stylish peach dress, and I can't help but wish I had my shit together like her. Ever since we left high school, she seemed to manifest men and money so easily. And here I am, struggling just to manifest a job. She wraps her arm around my neck. "Everything will work out, honey."

I sink into her warm embrace. Then I narrow my eyes as I feel her pity-pat my shoulder. "Sorry, ladies. I've got my Monday meeting shortly. Girl's night Friday?"

"Yeah, girl!" Fran chirps.

I nod and flash Piper a smile as she walks out of the cafe. Then I look at Fran. "Did she just pity-pat me?"

"She *so* did. We don't pity you though, okay? You'll get through this." Fran puts her hands on her stomach. "Phew, that chili dawg has got me all shook up. Could you watch the boys?"

"Of course," I reply.

"Thanks, girl." Fran eyeballs Niko and Andre, "You two be good for Aunty Sal. I'm just going to the ladies room."

"Yes, Mommy," they exclaim in unison. Fran leaves and I smile at the boys, who suddenly have mischief written all over their faces.

"Aunty Sal, we have this brownie?" Niko asks.

"Please?" Andre adds.

"Aw, sorry, boys. I would, but your mom said no chocolate. Sorry."

The boys cross their arms and screw up their little faces. As I raise my latte, Niko blurts out, *"Aunty Sal is 'motionally unstabled."*

My eyes widen in response. "What?!"

They giggle.

Confused by what I just heard, I lean in closer. "Say that again, Niko?"

"No!" Niko cheekily replies.

"Fine, I'll give you some brownie if you tell me."

"You 'motionally unstabled!" Niko says, laughing.

"Excuse me! How do you know those words?"

"Mama!" Niko chimes at the top of his voice.

Andre giggles and points his finger at me. "You have NO job. This why Mama pay for you lunch."

I am utterly astonished by these words that they shouldn't know at the age of four! They must be telling the truth. I can't believe Fran thinks this! I know I can be highly sensitive, but *emotionally unstable?* I huff and narrow my eyes. "Hey!"

The boys stop laughing. I extend my brownie toward them. "You want some?"

"Yes, yes," they chorus, clapping their hands.

Niko reaches across the table, but I withdraw the brownie. "On one condition."

Two small heads nod excitedly.

"It'll be our little secret," I say, with a finger on my lips.

They cheer gleefully, "We not tell, we not tell!"

I think back on past experiences where they ate chocolate cake. It didn't make them *that* hyperactive. One treat won't hurt them, and a deal is a deal, right? I slide the brownie across the table, and they gobble it up within seconds.

"Thank you, Aunty Sal, yummy!"

I lean across with a napkin and wipe the evidence off their faces. "You guys are *so* lucky you're cute!"

When Fran returns, the boys are bouncing off the walls like little gremlins.

"What the flaming hell is going on here?!"

I shrug my shoulders and rip the corner off the newspaper. "Hey Fran, something's come up. I've got to go."

"Um, okay. Do you need a ride?"

"No thanks, I'm emotionally stable enough to catch an Uber. Anyway, it looks like you have your work cut out for you," I smirk, pushing the cafe door wide. "Thanks for the brownie!"

"What has become of me?" I murmur, standing outside Happy Day Groceries watching someone dressed as a giant sausage hand out flyers.

I reluctantly walk into the store, and immediately my senses are overwhelmed. I hear the faint drone of dull music mixed with cash registers opening and shutting. Screaming babies and the crinkling sounds of potato crisps being stacked on shelves make me want to leave.

A tip I remember my mom giving me when I was job hunting straight out of drama school was to *always look at the employee's faces to see if they are happy, and if they are, it's a good place to work.* But all I see are dull, miserable workers that look like zombies have taken over their bodies.

I turn around to leave but a young man who looks no older than twenty is standing in my way, staring at me with a huge smile on his pimpled face.

"Hi! Welcome to Happy Day Groceries. My name is Jeremy!"

"Hiya."

"Didn't find what you were looking for?"

I try not to look directly at the unfortunate pimple on his nose. "Uh, not exactly."

"Well, we have a range of produce on sale today, including Maxwell's Meat discounted by twenty percent! What a bargain!"

"Ha, yeah. Total bargain." I inhale deeply. "Hey, so I heard you were hiring?"

Jeremy stops with his over-the-top act, and his voice changes to a less enthused tone.

"Great. Another one. Follow me."

I follow him to the back of the store and wait as he knocks on a door labelled *Helga Bottoms – Store Manager.*

A growly, raspy woman's voice that sounds like she's just smoked a packet of Camels yells through the door. "What is it?"

Jeremy opens the door. "We have another one, Helga."

"Great," she says with no effort to sound welcoming. She signals with a hand for me to come in. Jeremy leaves, but the smell of stale cigarettes stops me from going further. Helga is a solidly built, leathery-skinned woman in her late fifties. She resembles a scary clown, and I do not like clowns. Her flaming red frizzy hair with gray regrowth makes me think she needs to see a hairdresser, like, yesterday.

"Well! Don't just stand there, woman!"

"Oh, okay, ma'am." I close the door and take a seat.

"Looking for work, huh?"

"Yes."

Helga extends her hand. "Resume?"

"I know I should have brought it, but this decision was very last minute."

Helga withdraws her hand. "Right. Do you have experience as a checkout operator?"

"Um—no."

Helga raises one of her bushy eyebrows and makes a note on her coffee-stained notepad. I perk up. "But I can act like one!"

My nervous laugh dissolves after seeing Helga's reaction.

"Cute." Helga puts her pen down. "Why do people come here off the street with no experience thinking they can get a job? Do you think this job is easy?!"

"Um—no," I say, afraid for my life.

"Well, it isn't! Now stop wasting my time." She shoos me along with her hands and returns to her paperwork.

I audibly huff, rising from my chair. As I reach the door, the person in the sausage suit barges their way into the office with great force. I watch the young man struggle to pop his head out through the suit. I pinch my lips together, trying not to laugh as he reminds me of a baby pushing its way out of its mother. "I can't take it anymore. *I quit!*" he gasps.

A wide grin on Helga's face showcases her yellow-stained teeth.

I look at the horrendous sausage suit before casting Helga an appalled look. "Oh, no."

Helga nods. "You want a job or not?"

Chapter 6

Sal

"**M**AXWELL'S MEAT, COME GET *the meat you can't beat!*"

I hand out flyers and repeat the phrase in a monotone. If anyone were to recognize my voice, I would die of embarrassment. I don't know whether to cry or be grateful that no one can see me in such a monstrosity of an outfit. I can't believe I paid thousands of dollars for drama school to end up playing a fucking sausage. A sausage that, from different angles, looks like either a giant turd or a big wiener!

An hour goes by, and the scorching heat engulfs me. I can't breathe through the thick felt fabric that smothers my sweaty body. All I see is darkness except a glimpse of sunlight that shines through the two small holes near my eyes that help me navigate. I breathe slowly and search my brain for an affirmation to make me feel better. But I don't think any words or self-help guru can make me feel positive about this crappy situation.

I hand out some flyers to a friendly young family, then two boys that look like they are freshmen in high school ride up on bicycles.

"Hey, bruh! That's that Maxwell's sausage from TV."

"Oh, true bruh, it is too!" his friend replies.

As they move closer to me, my heart pounds against my chest.

"Hey Johnny, watch this." He holds up his middle finger in front of me. "Hey sausage, how many fingers am I holding up?"

I stand still, ignoring him.

The boy pokes me with his finger. "Hey, sausage! I asked a question."

His friend Johnny steps forward. "Yeah, don't be a rude sausage."

My stomach tosses and turns. Confrontation is something I always avoid. But when he pokes me again with more force and aggression, my impulse reactions take over and I kick him in the groin.

"Awww!" The boy bends over in agony while his friend Johnny laughs at him.

"Oh my gosh, I'm sorry!" I gasp.

"Shit, bruh! You got kicked by a *girl* sausage!" Johnny crows.

"I'm telling my mom on you!" The boy rides off doubled over with Johnny in tow, still chortling.

I walk into Helga's office with the sausage suit flopped over my arms and gently place it on the chair opposite her desk, where she reclines in the cool breeze from a fan.

"Thank you for giving me a chance, Helga."

As I turn to leave, Helga shows her warmer side.

"Wait." She walks to a dusty cupboard and ruffles through a bunch of blue and yellow uniforms. "I'd say you'd be a size six?"

I nod, and Helga throws me a uniform. "I can't have another one quit on me today. It looks bad for business. Put this on."

"Thank you, Helga. I won't let you down."

"Payment's minimum wage, paid every two weeks, but at the end of the week we let employees take expired food home."

"Two weeks!" I pause and soften my voice, "Is there any chance of an advance?"

Helga steps back and crosses her arms.

"Never mind."

I feel much happier in a uniform that shapes my figure and doesn't smudge my lipstick or ruin my hair. There is no way I will sabotage the only job I can get.

I stand beside Helga, paying close attention to how the cash register works, then I notice a long line of customers waiting to be served.

"Wow, it's so busy all of a sudden."

"You'll get that after school lets out. Every Tom, Dick, and Harry come to get their groceries." Helga bags a customer's groceries and wishes them a happy day. "All right, you got all that?"

"Easy! Scan the items, take the payment, and bag them up."

"And ..."

"Don't forget to smile and wish them a happy day."

"Well done. Always wish them a happy day. It makes them feel special." Helga whispers into my ear, "Even when they're not." She claps her hands together. "Right! Your turn."

A young lady places her groceries on the conveyor belt. "Good afternoon, ma'am," I say with enthusiasm and receive a smile back. After scanning through her goods, I bag them up. "Will that be all today ma'am?"

"Yes, thank you," the lady replies.

Helga leans into my ear. "Good job. Now ask if they're paying by cash, debit, or credit card. Remember, you must press this button if it's a credit card." Helga points to a selection of colorful buttons on the payment machine, which confuse my overwhelmed brain.

"This doesn't look like a normal payment machine. Why are there so many buttons?"

"That's because we haven't joined modern times. The payment won't go through if you don't press that button. If it doesn't go through, we don't balance at the end of the day, and it will come out of *your* pocket, not ours! Got it?"

"Got it."

I turn my attention to the lady. "How would you like to pay today, ma'am?"

"Debit, please."

The lady hands over her card, and I slide it through the machine while she enters her PIN. I glance at the machine. *Transaction Approved.* "Thank you. Have a happy day." My first happy customer leaves, and a sigh of relief leaves my chest.

"Not bad, Sally, not bad. Perhaps I underestimated you."

Three aisles down, Jeremy waves his hand frantically in the air and calls for Helga's attention. I know Helga can see him, but she looks the other way.

"Um, Helga, I think Jeremy needs you."

Helga lets out a raspy groan. "Useless! Do I have to do everything around here? I won't be long. Just keep doing what you're doing."

"Please don't go, Helga."

"It's easy! You'll be fine."

Panic rises in my chest as I watch her walk away, but when I see my next customer—a sweet-looking old lady—my quivering knees ease. Then my eyes flick to a tall man in his thirties with dusty blond hair and a stubbled jawline. He's dressed in a dark blue suit and carrying a lavish bouquet of flowers, and he's pushing his way to the front of the line!

"Excuse me, sonny!" grumbles the old lady.

"I'm sorry, but I'm running late."

His voice is just as I suspected. Arrogant, rich, deep. It's like his throat is laced with golden honey. Although I can't stand the man's audacity, I can't help but feel strangely drawn to his confident energy. Good-looking, arrogant men are my kryptonite. Which is probably why I'm still single. *But why does this one ooze so much delicious charm and smell so good?*

"Do you mind?" he asks the old lady, taking a fifty-dollar bill from his wallet.

The old lady happily takes it from him and blushes when he smirks at her. "Thanks, you're a darling."

I roll my eyes at Mr. Smirky-smirk. Who does he think he is, buying his way to the front of the line? But as soon as his ice blue eyes lock onto mine, my judgement takes a back seat and I put on my best smile. "Hi!"

He gestures back with a weak smile that just creases his dimples. "Sorry about that," he says, placing the flowers and a box of heart-shaped chocolates on the conveyor belt.

"Must be important?"

"It is," he says, letting out a discrete breath.

After I scan the chocolates, I pick up the flowers. "For me?" I jokingly ask, and laugh to make myself feel more comfortable, but it backfires.

"I don't mean to be rude, but can we please speed this up?" His cold tone prompts me to switch to professional mode.

"Yes, of course. Is that all today, sir?"

"Yes, thank you."

"Debit or cash?"

He glances down at the old lady swooning over his suit, "Well, I've given all my cash away." He looks back to me. "So it'll have to be credit, thanks."

Credit was the last thing I wanted to hear and hadn't included it as an option on purpose. He passes over his card, and I swipe it through the machine. I try to control my nerves while I figure out which button I'm meant to press.

"Everything okay?" he asks.

I look at him and gulp. "Yes! Would you like any gum with that?"

"No, that's all." He looks at his watch. I feel his urgency. Sweat starts dripping down my forehead, and my hands tremble.

"Is there a problem?"

Without making it obvious that I don't know what I'm doing, I glance over at Helga who's busy giving Jeremy a telling-off in front of his customers.

The man waves a hand in front of my eyes. "Well, did it go through?"

In distress, I press a button at random and hope my guardian angels are watching over me. After the longest second of my life, the words *Transaction Failed* appear on the machine.

I fire a fearful look at him, and his impatient eyes blast back at me. Panic mode sets in. Without thinking, I reply, "Yes! It did."

"Cheers." He flashes me a quick smile before he grabs his things and picks up his pace toward the exit.

Helga pulls into my view, shaking her head. "Sorry about that, Sally. Jeremy doesn't know the difference between a turnip and a freaking carrot!"

My worried gaze fixates on the man weaving his way through the customers. Helga looks in the same direction. "He sure is in a hurry. Any problems while I was gone?"

I refrain from looking at the payment machine. "Ah, no."

Helga looks at the failed transaction. "What happened here?"

Sweat melts from my forehead. "Oh, that! Um—"

"Well?"

I can't find any words. I stutter. There's no way I can afford to cover that man's elaborate items *or* to lose my job. "Uh … he just took off!"

"Without paying?"

My eyes bounce from side to side, and I slowly nod.

"Rats. We get these runaway food grabbers all the time." Helga grabs the radio that's clipped to her belt. "Lenny, we have a runner. I repeat, we have a runner."

The old lady places her groceries on the conveyor belt and shakes her head. "Why do all the good-looking men with money think they can have everything for free?"

My throat is too tight to respond. A sinking feeling squeezes my chest as I see the man rush out the door. Waiting for him outside is Lenny, the heavily weighted security guard, who tackles him to the ground like a WWE superstar. I gasp and follow Helga to the scene.

"Hey, what are you doing?" the man yells, blindsided by this sudden attack. His eyes project confusion and fear. Lenny puts him in an arm lock and pins him to the dirty ground. "Let me go!" he cries, struggling like a wriggly worm.

Helga looks down at the man while I peer out at him from behind her.

"Is this our thief, Sally?"

The breathless man looks up at me with puppy dog eyes that scream, *HELP ME!* I hem and haw while trying to figure out how I can get out of this giant pickle I've put myself in. Lenny loosens his grip around the man's neck.

"Well, go on! Tell them it wasn't me! I paid, right?"

"Well?" Helga asks, looking at me with razor-blade eyes.

My voice shoots out before I can stop it. "NO!"

"Yes, I did, you liar! Do I look like the type of guy who would steal?"

"That's enough, pretty boy," Lenny says, tightening his grip again.

"Alright, Lenny, keep him there until the cops come. Sally, come on, back to work."

I lag, walking behind Helga, full of shame. I peek over my shoulder and see him scowling at me with pure hostility. I mouth *I'm sorry*, which just seems to infuriate him and make the situation worse.

"You evil liar! I'm going to sue you for this!"

Chapter 7

Sal

AFTER A LONG AFTERNOON, Jeremy shows me how to lock up the store.

"Good job today, Sally. I'm sorry you had a runner on your first day."

"Thanks, Jeremy."

We walk to the parking lot, and he retrieves his bike. "Do you need a ride?"

I chuckle to myself. "No, thank you. My Uber's waiting for me."

"Cool as, see you tomorrow!" He rides off down the street, and I jump into the waiting car.

I gaze out the window, oblivious to the bright city lights among darkening skies, thinking about what a horrible person I am for letting an innocent man get arrested. A few minutes later we approach the local police station, which ignites a battle of conflicting thoughts in my overthinking brain.

"Stop!" I exclaim.

"What? Here?" the driver asks.

"Yes, here's perfect, thank you."

I click my heels up the concrete steps that lead to the front of the station. The smell of weed lingers from a homeless person sitting nearby holding a money pan. Knowing I don't have money to give away, I open my wallet and tip my loose change into his pan anyway. Although a selfless act, I do secretly hope that I receive good karma in return. After what I did to that poor man, I need all the good karma I can get.

I wait patiently by the information desk where a policewoman is having a casual conversation on the phone. I judge ten minutes to be long enough that I can press the bell again without seeming rude—I know I'm being ignored. The sound of the bell alerts the policewoman, who slides the phone to her neck.

"Yes," she says, sounding very bored.

"Yes, hi, me again. I want to know if a tall blond male, around say, thirty, came in today?"

The policewoman raises the phone to her ear, "I'll call you back." She reclines in her chair, unimpressed. "You're joking, right? Do you know how many of those types of men come through these doors every hour?"

"Right. Of course." I screw up my face, thinking. "What about a man dressed in a fancy suit who smells like Calvin Klein? He may be a little bruised and he would have been arrested about three pm—for stealing."

The policewoman tilts back her head and laughs. "Oh, you mean Sean Maxwell?"

My eyes widen, and a smile blossoms on my face. "Yes, that would be him!"

"Ah, what a hoot that was." The policewoman's laugh fizzles. "And who are you to him?"

Hmm, I clearly hadn't planned on getting this far. I twist my lips to one side. "Who am I to him?"

"We only let in visitors who are family."

What's one more lie. I try to project confidence. "His girl-friend! Yes—I'm his girlfriend."

She sits back in her chair and roams her eyes all over me. I smile at her, and she presses a button that opens the door next to her.

"You have five minutes."

"Thank you!"

The policewoman takes me down a long, cold, dark corridor that has several barred cells full of sad faces.

"Maxwell, your girlfriend's here!" she yells before giving me a stern look. "Over there. Remember, you only have five min-utes."

"Yes, of course."

I scan his cell, and he quickly gets up from the thin crusty mattress.

"Hi," I gently say, following with a little wave.

"You!" he responds with revulsion. He raises his voice, "That's not my girlfriend! Help, help, she's a psychopath!"

"*Shhh-shhh!* Please! I come in peace."

"Don't *shhh* me! You're the one who put me in here!"

"I'm sorry, I had to tell them I was your girlfriend, otherwise they wouldn't let me in."

"You've got some nerve, lady," he growls, lowering his voice.

"Are you okay? Have they treated you well?"

"Am I okay!? What do you think this place is, a day spa? No, I'm not okay! You've just ruined everything! Unless you're here to bail me out, you can leave."

"I would if I could, but that's why I lied today. It was my mistake and my first day on the job. I can't afford to lose it. You see, I'm an actress, but I—"

"Another aspiring actress whose dreams are crushed. Yeah, yeah heard it all before. Welcome to LA darlin'. Now, if you'll excuse me, I've got a wall to stare at."

"I just came here to say I'm sorry."

He grips the jail cell bars and raises his voice again. "Police, help! She's scaring me."

I wasn't expecting a warm welcome, but I didn't think he'd be such a man-child about it. I back away with both hands in the air. "Okay, okay, I'm leaving. Sheesh, you don't have to be such a jerk."

He sits on his bed, crosses his arms, and avoids eye contact with me. Worried that the police will catch me in my lies and put *me* in jail, I quicken my pace toward the exit.

"Asshole!" I mutter, as the door opens.

"Heard that!" he yells.

The next day I'm working the checkout, feeling more confident about my abilities. I make sure I'm on top of my game to avoid any more conflict. But the truth is, working the cash register reminds me of Sean and what a terrible person I am. I'm handing some bagged-up groceries to a customer when I notice a suspicious figure, face hidden by a cap, scanning the store through the window.

It's not until he catches my eye and smiles that I realize those devilish dimples are Sean's. I want to scream, but I know I can't make another scene. I tilt my body away from the window and continue serving customers. *Why is he here? Does he want revenge? Will he murder me or tell everyone what a liar I am?*

Seconds later, I hear tapping on the window. My mind tells me not to look, but my traitorous head doesn't listen. Slowly, I turn toward the window and see him waving at me like we're best buddies. *What the actual fuck?*

I close my eyes. *This can't be happening.*

I open them, and yep, it's totally happening.

He's signaling me to come outside! Before I can respond, he disappears and Helga's face pulls into focus.

"Everything going well, Sally? You look a little pale."

I sneak a glance over her beefy shoulders, where I can see the top of his cap. "Uh—yeah, I'm okay." I suck in a breath. "You know what, I haven't had a break yet. I think I just need to eat something."

"I didn't want to say anything, but you could do with some more meat on your bones." Helga hands me some brown paper bags. "After you restock these and take the trash out, you can take a ten minute break."

"Thanks, Helga."

I dump two big bags of trash in the garbage bins around the back of the store and smell my uniform, which reeks of rotten food. Tentatively, I look to each side for any sign of danger. Then I let out a sigh of relief at the sky.

"Looking for someone?"

I turn, following the deep voice behind me, and set my wary eyes on Sean. He's dressed in black sweatpants and a matching hoodie, standing with his hands in his pockets. I gather he doesn't want to be recognized, but he looks more like someone about to rob the place *now* than he did yesterday. "Sean?"

He nods, stepping toward me. I extend my hands, palms out. "Wait! This isn't a trap, is it? You know, the one where the guy lures the girl into an alleyway and kidnaps her?"

His charismatic laugh helps lower my heart rate. "No, I promise I'm not going to hurt you."

"Oh," I say, lowering my hands.

"Sorry to visit you at work, but I had no other way of finding you. I want to apologize for the way I reacted last night."

"It was my fault," I say contritely.

"Yeah, it kind of was," he concedes with a wry grin.

I look down at my pink cowboy boots, then up again to meet his earnest gaze. "I take it someone bailed you out?"

"My brother Derek. But I'd still be there if he thought no one would find out."

I smile and look around, trying to figure out something to say. Before it gets into awkward territory, Sean saves the day. "Your name's Sally?"

"That's me," I confirm, stepping toward him. My head barely reaches the top of his chest, and I can't figure out if my sudden adrenaline rush is because he's so cute or if I'm in danger.

"Nice name." He withdraws a hand from his pocket and extends it to me. I wipe my fingers on my uniform before letting his masculine hand swallow mine. Tiny tingles zap through my hand, exhilarating my body.

"So, you're an actress?"

"Was," I say, glancing at my watch.

"I won't keep you long. I know first-hand what a dragon your boss can be."

I laugh and twirl my hair around my fingers.

"I'll just come right out and say it then."

My thoughts run rampant as I puzzle over what the hell he's talking about.

"You're going to think this is strange, but I need your help," he sighs.

"Sure, anything. After all, I did get you arrested."

"Ah, how do I say this?" he hesitates, and I see his forehead scrunch up. "I was in such a rush yesterday because I was on my way to the airport to propose to my ... girlfriend."

My heart sinks a little. I have no idea why. Of course, a guy of his caliber has a girlfriend. Why else would he be buying flowers and chocolates? And why would he want anything to do with a girl like me?

"Oh my gosh! I am so sorry. Can't you ask her when she gets back from ... wherever?"

"It's complicated. She just got a job in New York. She told me that we'd be over if I didn't show up at the airport and agree to move with her."

I frown, not knowing what to think. "Oh, I see. You don't want to move to New York?"

"My business is here. I thought she would decide to stay if she had a ring." He smiles before continuing, "But I've got an even better plan."

"I'm not following."

"You said you're an actress, right?"

"Ye-ess."

"So, what do you think about acting as ... *my fiancée* for one night?"

"Woah!" I say as my mouth gapes open.

Sean raises his hands in a calming gesture. "I know, it's utterly ridiculous." His eyes swivel from side to side. "But what do you think?"

I take a giant stride back. "I think that *you're* the psycho now."

"Please, just hear me out. All I want you to do is have dinner with me at my parent's house. Once they approve of you, the deal's done, and you'll never see me again."

My eyes narrow. "Wait, what deal?"

"My dad announced his retirement yesterday. If I want half of the business, I need a fiancée. They're all about the wholesome family image, and well, I'm not known to be wholesome."

The endorphins I felt are replaced by a wave of raging anger. "Wow. And here I was thinking you genuinely came to say sorry." I shake my head. "I should know people like you are only nice when you want something. Story of my freaking life!"

"I'm sorry, I am. I was a jerk. But you got me arrested for no reason. That's on my criminal record now! I could have made them look at the video camera footage for evidence, but I didn't. You owe me!"

My rage seethes out at him. "Okay, no offense to my own feelings, but how does having a fiancée who works at Happy Day Groceries win them over?"

Sean rubs his temples. "That's where your acting comes in. You see, they have always wanted me to be with someone like—" he inhales deeply, "—a doctor."

"A doctor! How righteous of them. Your poor girlfriend, you were just going to use her, weren't you?"

"Ex-girlfriend. She's the one who chose her career over me. It worked out for the best. Our relationship was, let's say, not the healthiest."

"It sounds like *you* chose *your* career over *her*. Man, why are all the hot ones *such assholes?*"

He wiggles an eyebrow and smirks. "You think I'm hot, huh?"

My eyes narrow with disdain. "Not when you open your mouth."

Something occurs to me. "This doesn't make sense. Your parents would know I'm not your girlfriend."

"They've never met her. They don't even know her name. In fact, I know they wouldn't have even liked her. All they know is that I'm seeing someone. So, it may as well be you. Except you'll be a doctor. It's perfect! There's no way my parents won't approve."

I shake my head. "I am sorry about yesterday, but if you don't want to meet Lenny again, I suggest you leave. And please find another grocery store to shop at."

I walk away from him but stop when he speaks. "I'll pay you twenty thousand dollars."

I gasp and slowly spin around. "Twenty thousand dollars?! For one night?"

"Yes. One dinner. No strings attached."

Helga peers at me through the back window of the store. "Sally! Your break was over five minutes ago!"

"I'll let you think about it," Sean says, giving me a business card. He flips his hoodie up over the top of his cap and disappears, Clark Kent styles.

"Coming, Helga!" I tuck his card tightly in my front pocket and rush back inside.

Chapter 8

Sal

"**I**'M SCREWED!" I SAY, throwing a letter in the trash.

"Bad news?" Carlos asks, from where he's slumped on the couch holding a box of tissues.

"What do you care?" I snap, stalking to my bedroom with my little shadow, Oscar, on my heels.

"Danny broke up with me!"

I pause and try to act as if I give a damn. But I can only think about how I will pay my rent. "I'm sorry to hear that."

"I haven't been nice to you, have I?"

"Proceed," I prompt gleefully.

"No, that's all."

I resume walking toward my room.

"Okay, okay! I was jealous of you! That's why."

My eyes light up. He has my attention now. I walk straight up to him. "What? Me! No one has ever said that to me before. Thank you."

"Well, not so much your personality but more the physical part, if you know what I mean?"

I sit next to him. "Thank you! See, my friends think I overdo it. But we all need a bit of sparkle and pop in our lives, right? Oh, and just a tip, take the stairs. It tones your legs like no other."

Carlos sighs, nervously biting his nails.

"Carlos, are you alright?"

A tear escapes his eye, and I try to make him feel better. "Carlos, there are way better guys waiting for you out there."

"Okay, it's not your body as such. I want to be a woman!"

Memories of him wearing my lipstick flood back, and my eyes widen. "Oh my! Woah, it all makes sense now. Man, that's—"

"*Frustrating*. I'm a woman trapped in a man's body. It's not like I woke up and decided I wanted to be a woman. I think I was born this way. I've just been too scared to say it out loud. And when I finally told Danny, he couldn't handle it."

My face softens, and my loathing for him instantly vanishes. "I know how you feel. Sometimes I feel like I'm an intergalactic space alien trapped in a human body."

He looks at me and smiles. I place a hand on his shoulder. "I'm honored you told me. I think it's fabulous. Um, does this mean I should refer to you as 'she' now?"

"I don't think I'm ready for that yet. I'm still processing it myself."

"Got it. Sheesh, and here I was thinking you hated me because I sleepwalked into your room."

"Please don't ever do that again. I'm still not ready to remove the lock on my door."

"I'll try my best," I say, blushing with embarrassment.

"So, what will you do about your rent situation?"

"How do you know about that?"

"The landlord dropped that letter off today and wants his rent paid in fourteen days, or you're out. Sorry, his words, not mine."

I scrunch up my face, "I get paid in two weeks, so that'll cover half of what I owe." I relax into the couch and stare out the living room window. "I think I know what I have to do."

"What? Rob a bank?"

I return my gaze to him. "You won't believe what happened to me today. Get this! A stranger asked me to pretend to be his fiancée for a night!"

Carlos turns his whole head and gapes at me in wonder. "Oh hell, what are you, a whore?"

"*Right?* I told him no, of course."

"Good, always choose self-respect first."

In unison we sit back and cross our arms, then Carlos shoots me a sly look. "Was he going to pay you?"

"Twenty. Thousand. Dollars."

His eyes grow large.

"All I have to do is have dinner with his parents."

His eyes flick side to side then back at me, where I eagerly await his reaction.

"Do you *really* need self-respect right now?"

"No, not really."

"Who is this guy? Holy shitballs!"

I whip Sean's card out of my pocket and hand it to him.

"Sean Maxwell, hm." He does a quick google search and shows me a photo of Sean in a business suit. "Is that him?"

"Oh my god, that's him!" I grab the phone like a hungry child and greedily look at more photos. "I *can't* with all that jawline!"

"Jawline for dayyys," Carlos riffs with perfect timing.

When I scroll past a photo of him and his family, Carlos stops me and zooms in on the photo. "¡Dios mío! Noooo! He's the son of the Maxwells!"

"Huh?"

"You know, *Maxwell's Meat, the meat you can't beat!* Cha-ching!"

I take a closer look. "Oh my gosh, those are the people from the commercial."

"They are! My abuelo used to work for them when the company was just starting out. They're minted baby. Everyone knows them."

"Who knew there was money in meat." I consider. "What if they serve meat for dinner?"

"Bitch, it would be odd if they *didn't*. They're the Maxwells! What, you can't eat one sausage for *twenty thousand dollars*?" A teasing tone emerges, "Hell, you might even get *two* sausages if you're lucky."

"Ugh! Gross, Carlos. Please, don't talk about sausages right now. It's been a long day."

"What's in it for Sean?"

"Half his dad's company."

He shrugs his shoulders. "What have you got to lose?"

A retching noise escapes my throat. My shoulders tense and all the air rushes out of my chest. "I'm doing it!"

I punch his number into my phone and put it on speaker. "It's ringing!"

Carlos eagerly claps his hands, but stops when a deep voice answers.

"Sean here."

I freeze.

"Hello?" Sean asks.

Carlos slaps my arm, prompting me to say something.

"Hi! Sally here."

"Ahh, Sally, I was hoping you'd call. How are you?"

"I'm good."

"I take it you've thought about my offer?"

"One dinner, right? For twenty thousand?"

"Yes, yes, one dinner," he confirms with a low chuckle.

"Fine. You have a deal."

"Really? Thank you! That's amazing, *thank you*. I'll pick you up Friday night?"

"Sure."

"I'll send you a brief to memorize, so we come across as more believable. Just message me your address, and we're good to go."

"Um, okay."

"Sally, you've made me a happy man. I look forward to seeing you Friday."

I lower the phone and gape at Carlos.

"Holy shit, chica! You're going on a date with a millionaire!"

"A fake date, Carlos. What the heck have I just done?"

"You've just made yourself twenty thousand dollars richer!" He tries to high-five me, but I leave him hanging.

"I may have left out the part where I only get the money if his parents approve of me."

His hand drops. "Hold up. *Approve* of you?"

"And that's why he wants me to pretend to be ... a doctor."

"There's always a catch. Fucking millionaire snobs, they think they're so superior. Why can't you just be *you* the way you are?"

"It's okay. I can do this. I just have to consider it an acting role without the cameras. If I pull it off, it'll be the highest-paying gig of my life! Whatever gets me the money, right? Then I'll be able to pay all my rent and leave Happy Day Groceries. The only thing is ... well, I don't look like a doctor, do I?"

"Personally, I love your look. But *uh-uh* chica, we are going to have to tone all this *right* down. And those hair extensions *got* to go!"

"I was afraid you'd say that."

Carlos leaps off the couch like a ballerina and glides a hand toward his room. "What are you waiting for?"

"Now?"

"Mami, this make-over ... or make-*down,* I should say, is going to take a bit of time."

Beauty preparations go on long after nightfall, including exfoliating the fake tan off my body, a haircut, color, and blow-dry. Carlos applies a dash of makeup, then I am permitted to see his talent first-hand. "You ready, Sal?"

"If it means I can go to sleep, then yes."

He guides me to his full-length mirror. "You can look now."

Slowly I turn around, in suspense, like I'm about to find a gun pointed at my head. With one glance, one gasp, and one teardrop, a confident smile emerges on my face. My long Barbie locks are replaced with a style that lets my natural waves fall just past my ears. My formerly platinum hair is now a honey blonde with highlights that bring out my emerald green eyes. My makeup is classic and simple—just a little mascara and nude lipstick that softens my glowing skin.

"You like it?" Carlos asks.

Gently, I stroke my face. "Is that really me?"

"Sure is!"

"Wow. I look like a *woman.*"

"Some would say you could even pass for a *doctor*."

I grin from ear to ear. "Dr Sally is in the house."

Wednesday night means fried eggs on toast as I'm low on groceries and don't want to resort to the expired food Helga made me take home. While in the kitchen, I receive Sean's brief, which is, well, brief. It reads:

Name: Dr Sally Williams
Occupation: Doctor of Family Medicine
College: Albert Einstein College of Medicine
Address: 13 Riverside Dr, Burbank (with me—your fiancée)
Bio: Loves to cook and plans to someday raise a large family

Everything on that brief is nothing like me at all. Making pizza is my best culinary achievement, and although I like children, sometimes I feel I'm still one myself. Plus, there is no way I can afford them.

The idea of pretending to be a doctor without a script to memorize makes me shudder. Improv isn't what I excel at, but if you give me lines I can act my way out of anything. I know I'm emotionally intelligent, but I doubt my intellectual ability to pull this off. *What, actually, am I doing?*

I pace in circles, overanalyzing the situation in my head a million times. The more I think about how absurd this scenario is, the fainter I feel. I pick up my phone and make a call to Sean. After several rings I'm about to hang up, when he answers.

"Sally?"

"How did you know it was me?"

"I saved your number. I take it you got my brief?"

I press the bridge of my nose and remember to breathe. "Yeah, I did." I'm silent for a second, then blurt, "Sean, I don't think I can do this."

"Oh, I see."

His quiet tone makes me feel guilty. "I'm sorry."

"You can play a lawyer, an accountant, a vet—if that makes you feel better?"

I laugh sarcastically. "Wow, thanks so much! Man, you know how to make a girl feel special."

"I'm sorry. I suck at this. How about I come to your place, and we work on our story? If you're not comfortable by the end of our meeting, then I'll call the dinner off?"

"Fine," I say, massaging my forehead.

"Fine, as in, yes?!"

"That's what fine means, doesn't it?"

"I can never tell with women. Woah, you've got a bite to you." His cheeky tone becomes businesslike. "I'm just finishing up at the ranch. I can be at your place in two hours?"

"Sure, see you then." I end the call and run to rescue my burning eggs. *"Aw, man!"*

"Come in," I say uncertainly.

Sean smiles warmly and removes his muddy work boots before entering my apartment, which I appreciate. He dusts off his blue checked shirt and looks around my living room. "Nice place."

"Liar." But my dubious mood lightens at his attempt to be polite.

"It's not that bad," he says, laughing.

I'm trying not to stare at how his jeans hug his fit physique. "You look completely different when you're not in a suit."

Sean chuckles. "Good different, I hope. I feel like I'm going to choke wearing a tie." He stands still, looking at me. "Have you done something to your hair?"

I blush, running my fingers through my hair, downplaying the effort it took to create my new look. "A little."

"It looks great!" Sean is suddenly distracted by Oscar sniffing his feet. "Hello! Who's this?"

"That's my dog, Oscar."

Sean picks Oscar up and allows him to lick his face. I relax my shoulders and secretly enjoy Sean's affection for my pride and joy. "Can I get you anything?"

"No, I'm good, thank you."

"Shall we?" I guide him to the couch where I keep a healthy distance. "How are we going to do this?"

"First of all, I'm sorry I offended you before. I don't care what you do for a living. It's just my parents. Their idea of success is money and status."

"Well, as you can see, those are two things I certainly don't have. But I guess I could act as if I have them. However, this is different, like *a lot* different."

"You're right, it is."

With a resigned groan I say, "While I was waiting for you, I added some backstory."

"Great. Hit me!"

"My name is Sally Williams. *Dr* Sally Williams that is. I graduated from the Albert Einstein College of Medicine last year, and I'm now a family practitioner. After visiting my parents here in LA three months ago, I met you. We fell madly in love, and I've been visiting you at your Burbank condo every weekend since. I'm about to move back to LA and start my residency, in the meantime I'm organizing our wedding ... which is hypothetically *when* by the way?"

"I told Mom we haven't set a date yet. The longer we 'wait' the better."

"Got it. Oh, and two of my favorite things to do are cook and volunteer at the old folks home."

"Nice, yeah, yeah that's good. They'll buy that."

"So it's just you, your parents, and your brother Derek?"

"Yes, but you won't be meeting him. Thank God. How about you? Any siblings?"

"Nope, just me. I grew up with my parents in Santa Monica. I now live here with Oscar. Oh, and my roommate Carlos." I cross my legs and push my hair behind my ears. "I may have done a bit of googling on you."

"That's to be expected," he says with his smirky face.

"According to the internet, you work for your family's meat business as the ranch manager?"

"Something like that. I make sure all our livestock are properly grazed and looked after."

"And your brother is the marketing manager?"

"Uh-huh," he says, sounding bored.

"And now that your dad's announced his retirement, the role of CEO is up for grabs, and you want it?"

"Pretty much. But Dad's already said Derek will take over. He's the eldest and has a family of his own. They think he's perfect for the new face of the brand. But me, no! Never me." He sighs and leans closer. His strong jawline intimidates me as I listen to him intently.

"That's why you're going to help them see that I can do it. You're my last shot at this, Sally, before it gets signed over next week. Two hours of your time, that's all I ask."

I frown and look down, trying to think. Then I make my decision and grin up at him, shaking my head. "If I get busted, I'll find a way to put you back in jail."

Sean laughs and extends his hand. "Deal."

I look up at him through my lashes with wary eyes before I shake his waiting hand.

Chapter 9

Sal

FRIDAY ARRIVES, AND I'M now an expert at working the cash register. The bond I have built with Helga and my new colleagues makes me *want* to go to work. Plus, it keeps my mind off the looming anticipation of meeting Sean's parents in just a few hours. I'm determined to make them believe that I can be an asset to their family while proving to myself that I am an actress who can play roles other than 'bimbo.'

I've spent every waking moment not at work studying doctor's jargon. I've practiced walking with more grace, precision, and authority. I even created a voice that is much deeper: controlled and self-assured, things I am not.

Part of me wants to tell Fran and Piper about Sean and my new job. But what's the point? The relationship isn't real, and the job is nothing to write home about. This is my little secret. And it will all be over soon. In twenty-four hours, I'll get to move on to a new life! Err, whatever that looks like.

The clock strikes five, and I rush out of work in a flurry toward home. I shower, shave my legs, and blow-dry my hair, which now takes half the time due to my shorter style. I try on three disastrous outfits before changing into my pink fluffy robe.

Ding-dong! I hear the doorbell and spin my head around to scowl at my bedroom door. *That can't be Sean.*

"I'll get it!" Carlos sings at the top of his voice.

Moments later, Carlos pops his head into my room. "Only me."

"He's not here, is he?" I whisper.

"No, but this is." He pushes the door wide to reveal a large box wrapped in red ribbon. I carefully open it and pick up the fabric with my manicured hands. What unfurls before my heart-emoji eyes is a stunning white knee-length dress embroidered with lace, featuring a high structural collar.

"Wow, now *she's* a dress," Carlos says, admiring the details.

I check the label. "*I'm dead!* It's Valentino!"

Carlos pinches his fingers together in a vote of perfection. "I am *so* jealous right now!" he smiles. "Chop-chop, chica, we don't have much time!"

He sits me in front of my vanity mirror, finishes off my hair, and applies some makeup. This time, he does a bright red lip that stands out glamorously against the white of the dress. He crosses his arms and glares at me peacefully.

"Everything okay?"

"Sal, what's it like to be a woman?" he softly asks.

I snort and shake my head, not knowing where to begin. "Aw man, it's a freaking rollercoaster ride! For one, it's expensive. I spend every penny on hairdressers, waxing, diet pills, tampons, tanning, facial products, perfume, clothes, and makeup! And if I don't, I look like a sasquatch and then I get paranoid I'm not living up to society's expectations—let alone a *man's* expectations." I take a breath. "I'm a slave to my hormones, I constantly compare myself to other women, and I hate wearing bras!" I exhale a long silent breath and lighten my tone, "Apart from that, it's pretty cool. You'd love it!"

Carlos raises a dubious eyebrow and backs away. "Right ... I'll go pop a bottle of bubbles while you find your shoes."

"Thanks, Carlos. I could do with some liquid courage right about now."

As I finish getting ready I stare at myself in the mirror, in disbelief that the woman staring back is me. I hear Carlos outside my bedroom door, snapping me out of my indulgence. "Sal, are you ready yet?"

"I don't think I can do this!" I yell.

"Come on, come out and show me!"

I gingerly open my door and step out into the living room. Carlos's eyes travel from my red heels to my worried face.

"Man, I'm good," he mutters.

"You like it?"

"I totally *love* it! The only thing that needs changing is your smile."

As he hands me a glass of bubbles, my phone vibrates from inside my red clutch.

I peer at the screen and see a group message from Fran and Piper. "Oh my gosh."

"Who is it?" Carlos asks.

"I totally forgot about girl's night."

"Just tell them you're going on a date."

"I'm not telling them I'm going on a fake date! They already think I'm desperate." *And emotionally unstable!*

"Fine. Leave the fake part out."

I can't think about them right now, so I dash off a text that I have a better offer, wink emoji. I put my phone away and pace around the living room, rubbing my hands up and down my arms.

As I walk past the window, I stop. I squint my eyes, noticing a dark green Jeep Wrangler pull into the front parking lot. I expected him to drive a Merc or a Lamborghini based on his sleek professional look the first day we met.

Sean hops out of the car with a bouquet of flowers. Quickly, I sidestep to hide behind our faded brown curtain. "He's here!"

Carlos runs to the window. "Oooh-wee! *Hot damn!* Sweet Mother of Jesus, have mercy on my soul." Carlos flutters his fingers. "*Toodaloo!* What a delicious hunk of a man."

"Carlos! Get away from the window!" I sneak a peek through the window with one eye, and when I see him, I retract my head behind the curtain. "He is gorgeous, isn't he?"

"He sure is. And ... he's making a call."

I watch my phone ring.

"Well, answer it!" Carlos exclaims.

"Hi, Sean!"

"Hey, I'm here."

I compose myself and step in front of the window. I wave and he looks up at me with a cheeky, irresistible grin. "I'm coming down now," I say.

Carlos guides me away from the window and puts his hands on my shoulders. "Now, go act as you've never acted before and bring home that money, mami!"

I nod and grab my coat. "What if they don't like me? What if they find out I'm not a real doctor?"

"If you believe you are, then they will too. Repeat after me, *I am a doctor.*"

"I am a doctor. I am a doctor. I am a doctor." I take a breath. "You're right. I can do this." I bend down and air-kiss Oscar, grab my clutch, and make my way to the front door.

"If you don't answer your phone after eleven, I'm calling the cops!"

"Yup!"

I click my heels across the parking lot to where Sean's leaning against his car. One hand is in his pocket, and the other holds the bouquet. He is dressed in a white long-sleeved shirt rolled up to his elbows, and a leather belt holds up dark denim jeans that hug him in all the right places. His shiny black shoes tell me he's a man of class. The closer I get to him, the bigger his dimples grow. I notice his jittery fumbling as he changes stance and realize he's more nervous than I am!

"Hi, Sean," I say, trying to act confident.

He smiles and reaches for my hand like he's greeting a client. "Hi, Sally." The air between us grows with such intensity that we both laugh.

"I'm sorry, I haven't done this before," he says while his eyes linger over my dress.

"I can't believe *I'm* doing this."

"I can't believe *I asked you* to do this," he exclaims. "I have to say, stunning is an understatement."

I smooth my hair and blush. "Thank you for the dress."

"I'm just glad I got your size right. My parents are going to love you."

I bite my lower lip and turn my attention to the flowers. "For me?"

"They are for you ..." he says, and I feel my face light up like Times Square on New Year's Eve. He continues, "... to give to my mom."

Suddenly the lights go out. I try to mask my disappointment.

"Tiger lilies always make Mom smile."

"Oh. Yes, of course, makes sense. Why didn't I think of that?"

"I've also got a raspberry cheesecake in the car for you to give her. Now, if you could say you baked it yourself, that'll give you extra gold stars."

"Bring on those gold stars!" I laugh, masking my sudden outburst of doubt. But there is no going back now. He walks me over to the passenger door, which he opens like a true gentleman. I tense up, I've never had a guy open a car door for me before. *Cue the ominous soundtrack.*

"You promise you're not going to kidnap me?"

"I'll have you home by ten, cross my heart."

I slide myself into the Jeep and exhale before he jumps into his side. We look at each other for a long moment, and as he starts the engine, my heart starts to race.

We are quiet as he navigates through traffic until he gets onto the highway leading to Beverly Hills. His jittery thumb tapping on the steering wheel makes me squirm in my seat. He looks so serious when he drives. I like it. When he picks up speed to pass a car, my head turns to him. "You seem more nervous than I do. Should I be worried?"

"Yeah, sorry." He regains normal speed and loosens his shoulders. "I've got a lot riding on tonight, that's all. And it's not every day I bring a girl home to my parents." He briefly glances at me before returning his gaze to the road. "Was that your roommate waving at me before?"

"That would be him."

"I didn't think your boyfriend would approve of this situation."

"No way, Carlos is definitely not my boyfriend!"

Sean smiles. "We're nearly there, so if you want to pull out, let me know now."

"That's what he said," I murmur.

Sean gives me a questioning look.

"Relax, I'm here, aren't I?"

He sighs and jerks his neck from side to side. "Thank you. I'll ensure your efforts are well compensated."

"I guess we better get to work then!" I rub my hands together. "Right! How old are you?"

"I turn thirty-four in November. You?"

I hesitate before answering. "I turn the big three-zero on July fourth."

"Independence Day huh! Not long now before the wrinkles creep in."

Wrinkles! What wrinkles? I sneak a peek at my reflection in the wing mirror.

Sean grins, watching me. "I was joking!" He continues, dropping the tease, "You have nothing to worry about."

I narrow my eyes and smile. "Boxers or briefs?"

He raises his eyebrow and laughs. "What kind of question is that? Gee, you're not shy, are you!"

"Believe it or not, the little details make us more believable. Trust me. I'm the actor here."

"Briefs it is then."

"Phew! Good choice. Rock or country?"

"Country."

"Okay. Who would you rather date, Britney Spears or Beyonce?"

He laughs. "Can I say neither of them?"

"Really! What guy wouldn't want to date them? They're total babes. I'd love a booty like Beyonce."

"Nah, I'm more of an eye-man myself. Anyway, I think you've asked enough questions. It's my turn. What's your deepest fear?"

Dumbfounded, I give him a blank look. I didn't expect a profound question like that.

He prompts me, "Okay, is it spiders, needles, sharks?"

None of Sean's suggestions is my fear. It's either being alone or being with someone who makes me feel alone. I do know my fear of rejection stops me from letting anyone get to know the real me. But he doesn't need to know that. "Spiders! Definitely, spiders."

"Favorite food?"

"Hands down, pizza."

He lets out a hefty chuckle.

"What? Who doesn't like pizza?"

"It's just refreshing not to hear 'salad' or 'sushi' like every girl I've dated around here."

"Maybe you're dating the wrong girls, then."

His devilish smile makes me melt into my seat. He's a lot more approachable than I thought he would be. I look out the window and admire the luxury villas and grand mansions that pass my starry eyes. "Wow!"

I look back at Sean, and one corner of his mouth curls. "Not bad, huh? This is where I grew up."

"Lucky you."

When we turn into a street signposted Hillcrest Road, Sean starts doing his tapping thing again on the steering wheel. Then, he pulls the car over to the side of the road.

"What's wrong, Sean?"

He gulps. "That's my parents' house." He points to a se-cluded house visible behind mature trees and a security gate. I can just see ivy lining the exterior of the three-story home that people like me only dream about.

"Um, Sean, I have to tell you something."

He snaps out of his trance and looks at me. "Please don't tell me you're a man."

I place one hand on my stomach to help control the laughter that's so contagious he joins in.

"No, I'm a ... vegetarian."

His laugh fades into a sigh. "Oh, I see."

"I know it's not ideal. The last time I ate meat was when I was twenty-two, and it didn't agree with me. Plus, the thought of eating animals freaks me out."

Sean screws up his mouth. "I'm sorry, I shouldn't have as-sumed. But this could be a problem."

I look down and twiddle my fingers.

"I mean, I don't care, but if you're 'hypothetically' going to be the wife of a Maxwell and therefore a face of our brand, yeah, that's a big problem."

I observe Sean, he's in deep thought. I feel terrible that I didn't say anything sooner. "You know what, I'm sure eating meat for one night won't hurt me."

He rests his hand on my shoulder. The warmth of his touch sends tingles down my arm.

"Thanks, but if you don't eat meat, I'll have to figure some-thing out." He takes his hand off my shoulder and makes a slight groaning noise. "I've got to warn you, my dad can be a bit of a stickler, so don't take things personally."

"How can I when I'm pretending to be someone else."

"Oh, I forgot." He leans across me, and a whiff of his masculine cologne caresses past. He opens the glove compartment and pulls out a Tiffany box.

"How could I forget this bad boy," he lifts the lid, and my eyes sparkle in the flashes of light thrown off the huge emerald-cut diamond.

Even though it's just a pretty prop, judging by the way my heart pelts against my chest in a flurry, it's the most beautiful thing I have ever seen.

"You like it?"

I downplay my excitement. "I'm more of a princess-cut kind of girl."

He responds by raising an eyebrow.

"Of course, who wouldn't love it!"

"In that case, Sally, will you be my fake fiancée for the night?"

"I will," I say, extending my hand without a thought.

As he glides the ring up my finger, electricity shoots through my hand, and the butterflies in my belly take flight in anxious anticipation. Our eyes lock, and we share a solemn nod before Sean starts the car for the show that's about to begin.

Chapter 10

Sal

DING-DONG! SEAN AND I stand side by side, anxiously waiting for his parents to open their front door. I hold the flowers in one hand while Sean holds the cheesecake. I suck in a rush of air, and Sean extends his hand which I gratefully accept. Then, I watch the front door open in seeming slow motion. I squeeze his hand so tight it makes him smile.

"Hi, Mom."

"Hello, darling!"

His mom's eyes look straight through me. "And who do we have here?"

"Mom. I'd like you to meet Sally," he swallows. "My fiancée."

I put on the sweetest smile I can muster. But I am *so* intimidated by her presence. Madeline Maxwell is a woman of refined taste; she wears a long-sleeved Givenchy dress that falls to just below her knees. Her perfectly styled gold jewelry punches my eyes. Her silvery-blonde hair bounces just above her shoulders, and although I can tell she's had some work done, she looks younger than I anticipated.

"Welcome, Sally. I'm Madeline," she says warmly. But I can tell she's hiding her bemusement over this new courtship.

"Pleased to meet you, Madeline." I proffer the flowers. "These are for you."

"Tiger lilies! Did Sean tell you these are my favorite?"

"He may have," I say, grinning at Sean.

Sean hands his mom the cheesecake. "Sally baked you this."

"Oh, how wonderful. A girl after my own heart. Come in. We have lots to catch up on."

Madeline ushers us into her elegant entryway, where Sean takes off my coat and hangs it on a porcelain hook near the foot of a wide staircase that spirals upwards.

"Where's Dad?"

"Oh, you know what your father's like." She looks at me, "Not a man of many words."

We follow Madeline through to the living area, which is rimmed by large windows that allow filtered light to accentuate the extravagant paintings mounted on the almond white walls. Sheer, pale green curtains frame the decorous furniture and Persian rug.

Beyond the windows the pool glistens, surrounded by half an acre of well-kept lawn and gardens that look like they belong in a home design magazine.

"Your home is impeccable, Madeline. I just adore the way you've styled it," I say, putting on my well-practiced superior voice.

"Oh, thank you Sally."

A man in his early seventies dressed in a checked shirt and a velvet green jacket with a hanky in the front pocket appears in the living room doorway.

"Clifford, you've come to join us!" exclaims Madeline.

Sean moves closer to me, and I see him adjusting his shirt. "Hey, Dad," he says.

Clifford ignores him and stares at me like I'm an intruder. With a big pearly white smile, Madeline strides up to Clifford. I can see her smile change as she angrily whispers at him.

Aware of the sudden mood change in the room, I sense I have to be the one to sprinkle a little grace and charm. I confidently glide toward Clifford and extend my hand.

"Hi, Mr. Maxwell. I'm Sally." Clifford reluctantly shakes my hand, and his suspicious eyes meet mine.

"No need for those formalities here if you're going to marry our son," he says with a hint of passive aggression.

"Clifford it is!"

Madeline hands Clifford the cheesecake and flowers. "Be a dear and put these in a vase and fetch the champagne, would you?"

Sean catches Clifford's attention as he leaves the room. "And some water please, Dad." Clifford answers him with a regal nod.

Gracefully, I float around the living room and rest my gaze upon some framed family photos and trophies. Most, if not all, of the trophies have Derek's name on them. However, I'm more interested in knowing about Sean. "Sally, you can come sit down if you like," Sean says from the couch.

I smile and ignore his gesture. My eyes single out a photo of Sean and his brother when they were young, standing in the middle of some farmland, hugging a cow. "Oh my, is this you, Sean?!"

"Great, here we go," Sean mutters.

Madeline joins me around the photos with enthusiasm. "Wasn't he a chubby little thing? He got so round at one stage that we had to hide the twinkies and put him on a diet."

"Mom! Please!" Sean exclaims.

I look over at Sean and press my lips together. "You didn't tell me that, darling."

Sean groans, and Madeline smiles. "I think we hit a sore spot, Sally."

Clifford enters the room with the bottle of champagne and a carafe of water and places them on the table beside Sean. "Thanks, Dad."

Madeline continues talking, pointing to the photo. "That was his favorite steer. He even named it. What was his name again, Sean?"

"Mom. Seriously, no one cares."

Clifford seems to remember it vividly. "Freddy. You named him Freddy, son."

"He's adorable!" I say, glancing across at Sean as he pours the champagne into flutes.

"Thanks, babe," he replies.

"I meant Freddy, darling," I wink at him and return my attention to the photo. After all, the more I talk about them, the less they talk about me.

"Was this photo taken on your ranch, Clifford?"

"One of them. We have many ranches across several states. We are proud that all our farm stock is grass-fed and completely free-range."

"I'm happy to hear that. Grass-fed meat is much healthier for the heart."

"You would know, being a doctor."

Sean clears his throat. "Champagne, anyone?"

We all join him and take a glass. Sean goes for the water, and I'm intrigued. "Not drinking, darling?"

Sean's eyes subtly flicker at Clifford. "Not tonight."

I can tell by his voice that he doesn't want me to press him about it. And neither does Madeline, who quickly raises her flute in the air. "Cheers, everyone! Sally, welcome to our home." We clink our glasses, and just as I'm about to take a sip, my eyes catch Clifford staring at me.

"Forgive me, Sally. But you look a little young to be a doctor."

"Clifford, you charmer! Thank you, but I'm not that young. It's taken me eight years of study, and the learning never stops. This is my first year out of med school, so I'm starting my residency soon."

"What field do you specialize in?"

"I'm lucky to be able to specialize in my passion, family medicine. Family is everything."

"Oh, how wonderful!" Madeline exclaims, giving Sean an approving look. Before I can go on, I'm interrupted by the sound of their doorbell.

Madeline puts her glass down. "Well, who could that be? You weren't expecting anyone, were you, Clifford?"

He shakes his head. Madeline rises from her seat. "Excuse me one moment."

Sean and I share a look filled with apprehension. Apart from an exchange of weak smiles, no one moves or says a word. The silence is interrupted by the strong presence of a man who looks like an older version of Sean, although shorter, and with dark hair that's receding. *Oh yay, this must be the brother.*

"Hey, Dad!" the imposter exclaims.

Clifford raises his glass and offers him a nod. "Son."

"Derek?" Sean says, clearly taken aback by his presence.

His eyes dance back and forth between Sean and me. "Brother dearest!"

Sean stands up, clenching his fists. "What are you doing here?"

"You don't look happy to see me, and after I bailed you out? How rude."

Madeline calls from behind Derek. "Boys! Not in front of our guest, please."

"It's alright Mom, we'll play nice." His attention turns to me. I don't know how I will improvise my way out of this situation. All I can do is keep a controlled composure.

"How brash of me! Who is this fine specimen?" Derek kisses my hand, and I try not to squirm. Like seriously, are we in the eighteenth century suddenly? *Who kisses on hands and casually likens women to scientific trophies?*

"Hi, I'm Sally."

"So, you *are* real."

Sean moves closer to me. "Derek, if you don't mind, we—"

"It's alright, brother. I was just passing by after a long day in the office. I'm not staying long. I just had to come over to see for myself." He studies me. "And here she is! My little bro has finally grown up."

"We have enough food if you'd like to stay?" Madeline asks.

Oh, boy. Here we go. *What the freaking heck!*

Derek looks at Sean, who's eyeballing him with rage. "Oh no, Mom, I shouldn't," Derek says.

"Where're Victoria and Katie?" Sean asks.

"With the in-laws, so I'm flying solo tonight."

Clifford chimes in with a low authoritative voice. "Stay for dinner, son. It'll give us all a chance to get to know Sally better."

"No, that's okay, Dad. I'll get takeout. I don't want to intrude."

"Another time then," Sean says, but his hint is dismissed.

"Oh, go on then. You guys twisted my arm. I'll stay if that's alright with you, Sally?"

"Of course," I reply, doing a stellar job of suppressing my nerves.

Derek squeezes himself between Sean and me. "This is comfy, isn't it? Wine o'clock, I see? Don't mind if I do." As he leans forward to pour himself a glass, Sean gives me a comforting smile.

Derek leans back into the couch. "So, Sally, Mom told me you're a doctor?"

"I am! We were just talking about that, funnily enough."

"Where did you study?"

"Albert Einstein in New York."

"No way! I have a buddy who went there. What year did you graduate?"

"Last year."

"Get out of town! So did he. You'll know Tom Reilly then?"

Fuck!! My eyes grow wide, and a flush of dread heats my face. "Tom Reilly. Hmm. Gosh, it was such a big class."

"Seriously, you can't miss him. Bright red hair, glasses, complete nerd alert!"

I scan the room to see all eyes awaiting my response. "Oh! *Tom Reilly*. Yes, of course. I met him a few times. I've never been good with names. Nice guy. Very intelligent man."

"What's your last name? I'll let him know I met you."

I glance at Sean, who's keeping his composure. "Williams," I reply.

"Soon to be Maxwell, I hear." Derek takes a sip before continuing. "So, you left New York for my brother? That's a risk!"

"Derek!" Madeline exclaims, seeking support from Clifford, who seems content to listen more than he talks.

"What? I'm not used to seeing him with someone who has brains, someone who isn't wearing a T-shirt as a dress and a paint palette as a face."

Madeline politely addresses me. "What he means, dear, is that it's nice to see Sean with someone who has a bit of class finally." Madeline looks at Sean. "We're not used to you bringing girls home for dinner, are we Sean? I knew you were seeing someone, but you didn't mention she was a doctor!"

"Trust me, my brother's never made smart decisions regarding girls, so why start now, I wonder?" Derek puts his finger on his chin.

I can already see hints of why I am here. I clear my throat. "I know Sean to be very intelligent. But his kindness was what attracted me to him initially."

The corner of Sean's mouth curls and his eyes soften like blueberry-swirl ice cream left in the sun.

Derek darts beady eyes at his brother. "How *did* you two meet anyway?" His eyes shift to me. "Because up until three days ago, we didn't know your name, and now you're getting married? A little odd, don't you think?"

Clifford finally speaks up. "Quiet son, let them tell us."

Sean declares, "Derek, you know I've been seeing someone for months. I just didn't say who because I wanted to be sure it was serious. And now I am." He looks at me and smiles. "Do you want to tell the story, Sal? You do it better than me."

"Certainly, darling," I simper and lean across Derek to rub Sean's shoulder before I address everyone. "It's truly a boring story, I must warn you."

Madeline twinkles her fingers in the air. "Go on. We want to hear it."

I clasp my hands together. "Okay, so I was visiting my parents here in LA about three months ago, and I was in a grocery store of all places. I was cooking spaghetti bolognese for my parents." I pause. "They just *love* Maxwell's Meat, by the way!" Madeline gasps with appreciation, and Clifford leans in closer.

"So, I was down the meat aisle and I saw there was only one packet of Maxwell's ground beef left, as I reached out to grab it—behold—a big, hairy, masculine hand snatched it from under my nose."

Madeline squawks indignantly.

"I know, Madeline, I know," I say, grinning confidently at Sean. "I look up, and this tall, handsome stranger looks back at me with big, beautiful, blue eyes that pierced my soul like daggers." I hold my breath and, at the same time, hold everyone's attention. "And that's when it happened. He not only stole my meat that day, he stole my heart."

Madeline wipes a tear from her eye, and Derek puts his finger in his mouth, pretending to gag. "Who got the meat in the end?"

"Do you have to ask, big brother?"

"If you had your way, you would have taken it."

I chime in. "No. No, Derek, he gracefully gave it to me." I point a finger in the air, subtly flashing my diamond at the same time. "But on one condition!"

They all lean in closer. Wielding them like I would any audience, I pause for dramatic effect. "That I give him my number."

Madeline laughs with delight, and Clifford shows signs of loosening up. "That's my boy."

Sean smiles warmly at his dad while Derek hastily crosses his arms. I hear him mutter, "Charming."

"It was!" I smile brightly at Sean. "Ever since then, I've been flying back and forth for weekends, and we thought—"

Sean interrupts me and extends his arm across Derek to hold my hand. "We thought—*let's make it official*. I asked her to move in with me, and here we are."

Madeline claps her hands. "That is a wonderful story!"

Derek's disgruntled eyes look down at our hands, and he watches us swoon over each other like we've been in love for years.

The beeping sound of an oven timer invades the room. Madeline springs to her dainty feet, "I hope everyone's hungry!"

Chapter 11

Sal

THE PUNGENT SMELL OF meat dominates the sweet aromas of garlic and sage as Madeline carries her meatloaf to the elegant white table that we are seated around.

An array of mouthwatering dishes are laid out, including roast vegetables, peas, garlic bread and mashed potatoes. A lavish crystal chandelier hangs above the middle of the table, creating a warm sparkly ambience. Madeline sits at one end of the table, opposite Clifford who is tucking a napkin over his shirt.

Derek sits across from Sean and watches him whisper into my ear. "You're doing great."

I smile and look across at Derek's surly demeanor.

Madeline puts her hands together in a prayer position. "Sally dear, would you like to do the honors?"

"Oh. Certainly, Madeline." My eyes flicker around the table and see everyone close their eyes. Sean gives me a nod before he closes his. I put my hands together and clear my throat.

"Dear God, thank you for our glorious food. May the meat killed for our benefit be sent to our holy heaven and bless our bellies with great health and fortune. May all the animals on the planet, including all the insects and rodents, be—" I abruptly stop when I feel Sean kicking me under the table. I open my eyes, and he's shooting me a look that I translate as *what the fuck are you doing?*

I quickly wrap up the prayer and make a mental note to stay in character. "Please bless this lovely food, may it nourish our bodies. Amen."

When I open my eyes, Derek's narrow eyes stare back at me.

"Thank you, Sally. That was ... lovely. Very scientific. Dig in, everybody!" Madeline says.

Plates of food are passed around the table. I put a healthy serving of roast vegetables on my plate, accompanied by garlic bread and a colossal dollop of mashed potatoes, so there isn't much room for anything else. Derek seems particularly interested in my plate. My nerves are kicking in, and I wish he would stop watching my every move. He picks up the meatloaf dish and offers it to me. I hesitate.

"Don't tell me you're one of those to-fu-eating so-called *woke* hippies?"

I hear cutlery being placed on the table, and suddenly all eyes are on me. Sean stalls his first forkful and clenches his jaw. I extend my plate over to Derek. "I find it insulting that you asked. I was saving the best till last. Bring it over here! Yum, yum!"

I shoot a brief sideways glance at Sean, but I can tell he doesn't know how to get me out of this. The only thing I can do is eat it like a champ and pray to the bowel gods for a clean exit. I dance around the meat with my fork and take a bite of mashed potatoes. "Mm, these are so good!"

Madeline smiles. "Thank you, Sally. Cooking, I must say, is one thing I don't require help with. Now, I hear you're a great cook?"

"I think Sean's just biased."

"Well, your cheesecake looks fantastic. How did you make it?"

My mouth opens, but no words come out. I have never thought about what ingredients go into a cheesecake. "Oh, with raspberries ... cheese and a little bit of cake."

Madeline and even Clifford, laugh.

"Funny *and* smart," Derek says with sarcasm before forking some meatloaf into his mouth.

"I know it's early days, but have you talked about kids yet?"

Clifford casts a stern look across the table. "Madeline!"

"They're not getting any younger, Clifford," Madeline replies.

Sean's eyes roll. "Yes, Mom, of course we have."

"How many?" Derek abruptly asks.

Sean and I look at each other. Then we respond in unison, but I blurt out 'two', and Sean says 'four.'

Derek tilts his head to the side. "Well, which was it, two or four?"

I place my hand on Sean's leg. "Remember, darling. We said we'd start with two, and if we thought we could manage our busy careers, we would consider two more."

Sean points his fork in the air, and I can tell he's pretending to 'remember.' "That's right, I recall now," he says.

"How delightful! We've always wanted lots of grandchildren, haven't we, Clifford?" Clifford grunts, chewing his food.

"Mom, that meatloaf was so good!" Sean reaches across to my plate and poaches my portion.

Clifford steeples his fingers. "Sean Maxwell, where are your manners?"

Before Sean responds, I intervene. "It's okay, Clifford. He does this all the time," I laugh before turning to Sean. "Fine, you can have mine but just this once."

Sean kisses me on the cheek and then returns to eating. Even though I know it was a fake kiss, the warm glow and tingles I feel on my face give me the inspiration I need to get through dinner.

Derek narrows in on my plate again. This man does *not* give up. "Here, have mine, Sally."

"That's okay, Derek," I say, hoping he backs off.

"I'm the one who gate-crashed this dinner. If anyone should go without, it's me."

Clifford smiles at Derek "That's kind of you, son."

Sean scowls and shakes his head.

Derek leans over and places what's left on his plate onto mine. "Besides, you're not a true Maxwell until you've had a home-cooked Maxwell's cut prepared by"—he jerks his chin in Madeline's direction—"the matriarch herself."

I receive an encouraging smile from Madeline, and I have no other option than to accept his gesture. "Of course, thank you."

I'm face to face with the meatloaf, and my feet start to tap like they would right before a big audition. Sean gently puts a hand on my leg and this instantly calms me. We share a secret glance, then he loosens his collar. He's starting to feel the pressure and I can't let him down. Eating a little bit of meat is the least I can do for such a large sum of money. Perhaps it won't affect me this time. Either way, I'm about to find out.

I can smell the thick odor of animal fat and glance around the table. All eyes are on me. "Mm, smells so good!" I widen my eyes in excitement and carve out a small bite. As the meatloaf reaches my mouth, I know this is a moment that could make or break the deal. I force myself to eat it, and I pretend it's pizza so it's more tolerable. I hum and ahh with appreciation. "*Sooo good!*"

Everyone looks relieved, but most of all Sean, who unclenches his jaw.

Clifford musters a smile to see me enjoying my food. "I'm telling you, it's meat you won't beat," he says unironically.

"I can see why!" I exclaim, forcing another bite into my mouth as naturally as possible without gagging.

"It's not just the meat, Dad. It's marketing. Our revenue wouldn't have grown over thirty percent if I hadn't stepped in," Derek states arrogantly.

Sean rolls his eyes and pays me extra attention while I continue eating.

"Yes, son, and we are very grateful." Clifford half raises his champagne in Derek's direction, and Derek's pleased smile turns to me.

"And Sally, that's why this time next week you will be looking at the new CEO of Maxwell's."

Sean slams his knife and fork down on the table, and my stomach makes a gurgling sound.

"It's not official yet, is it, Dad?" Sean presses, with fire in his voice.

Clifford clears his throat. "I think this is a discussion for another time."

Derek crosses his arms. "We've talked about this, Sean. I have a family who can promote the happy family Maxwell brand. You're a bachelor who tells girls you're a cowboy so you can get laid."

Oh my gosh, who is this guy?! I politely interrupt, "*Was* a bachelor."

All eyes turn to me as I place my hand on Seans shoulder. I remain composed, even though the somersaults in my lower bowels are raising my temperature.

Derek ignores me and addresses Sean, who looks ready for war.

"You're better visiting the farms where no one can see you, Sean."

Madeline rubs her temples, Clifford takes another bite, and I contract my lower body muscles to quiet an array of rumbling noises.

Sean throws his napkin onto the table. "How long are you two going to punish me? It was *one* mistake!"

Derek raises a finger in the air. "One mistake that not only lost us revenue but our reputation. Do you really think marrying someone you hardly know will change the fact that you're not CEO material!?"

The heavy tension in the air is suddenly diverted by a series of short desperate gasps from Clifford. *Choking* types of gasps that send my heart to my feet.

"Clifford! Not at the dinner table, please," Madeline barks, unaware that her own husband looks like he's dying. I can tell he wants to speak, but his hands are clutched around his throat.

"Mom, he's choking!" Sean says, rushing to his side. He gives Clifford three big blows to the back. We all wait. Nothing.

Derek's eyes ambush me with fear. "Well, you're the doctor! Do something!"

Fuck, fuck, double fuck! I can feel my face go as pale as Clifford's, and all I want to do is cry. The only things I know about saving someone from death-by-choking I learned from TV medical dramas.

Madeline rises from her chair. "Quickly, Sally!"

I rush to Clifford, whose eyes are bulging, and push Sean aside. "Sal, what are you *doing?*" he mutters through gritted teeth.

"Move out of my way, Sean!" I position my petite body behind Clifford, flapping his arms around like a lifeless bird unable to fly. As soon as I'm in position, I perform an abdominal thrust that barely jiggles his collapsing body. With greater force, I do it again, and I hear an agonized sound from him like a wounded wildebeest hanging on to dear life.

"He's turning blue!" Derek screams.

"Sal, give him to me," Sean says, his tone more serious than ever.

With all the effort I can muster, I try again. "Come on, Clifford!" I thrust as I have never thrust before. A tiny piece of dislodged meat shoots across the room and lands on Madeline's plate. She lets out a squeamish yelp. My stomach tightens and I clench my fists. *Oh, shit.* Then my eyes widen when I realize that might be literal.

I wipe the sweat from my forehead with my hand and step back while Sean, Derek and Madeline hover over Clifford, who's catching his breath.

Sean's astonished eyes are riveted on me like I'm Mother Teresa. "You did it!"

Still in shock, I hesitantly smile. "Um ... where's the bathroom?"

"There's one off the living room," Sean says, looking at me in awe.

"That one doesn't flush properly, dear. You're best to go upstairs," Madeline says automatically, stroking Clifford's back.

Sean steps toward me. "Come, I'll show you."

I extend both my palms. "No!" I lighten my tone. "I mean—no, you should stay with your dad. He's been through some trauma. It's crucial that he is with his family."

Madeline clasps her hands under her chin. "Aww! Thank you, Sally."

I offer her a confident nod like I have done this many times. "You're welcome. The oxygen in his brain will fill up again, so let him rest for a few moments, and his vital signs should return to normal."

Swiftly, I grab my clutch, flash Sean a quick smile and leave the room as naturally as I can without letting them see me from behind. After all, I have no idea how bad the damage is.

Chapter 12

Sean

"Y OU OKAY DAD?" I ask.

My dad takes a while to respond. Then I see his face melt into a picture of enlightenment. "I saw the tunnel of light, and it was … beautiful."

Skeptical glances flit between myself, Mom and Derek. Dad flashes a reverential smile at me, "She saved me, Sean."

"Isn't she wonderful?" Mom exclaims.

"I take it I have your approval then?" I ask.

Dad looks at Mom, they both radiate joy. "Yes, son, you have our approval."

Suddenly I'm grinning so hard it hurts. "I knew you'd love her!"

Derek scowls at me dangerously. "Hate to break up such a memorable family moment, but what does this mean?"

Dad turns his attention to Derek. "It means I think Sean is ready to redeem himself. If he feels he's ready, then it's only fair to split the CEO role."

My grin grows wider.

"What about what happened last year Dad?! We can't risk our reputation being ruined again after I've spent the last eight months rebuilding it."

"Son, I was just moments away from meeting my maker. There's no time to keep reliving the past. The decision has been made."

Derek sulks on his chair like a naughty boy in time-out before raising his voice in protest, "He doesn't have a family, or kids! He's not even married yet!"

Sal

I open many doors along the beautiful hallway before I find the bathroom, the discovery bringing colossal relief. I ruffle up my dress, sit on the toilet and let out a whimpering cry. After I wash my hands, I look over my shoulder and gasp at an unflattering stain below my panty line. Although it's a small spot, it stands out against my white dress.

I slip the dress off, grab a washcloth and a bar of soap and scrub as if my life depended on it. To my delight, the stain is removed. All that's left is a wet patch. I put the dress back on and open the window to let fresh air in. As I stand at the window I contemplate the thick ivy lining the exterior of the house. *Cue the genius escape plan!*

Suddenly, I fully believe I can climb down the ivy and catch an Uber out of here! I can't face seeing the Maxwells again after this code-brown situation and will gladly work at Happy Day Groceries for the rest of my life to be spared that particular indignity.

After brief contemplation I tuck my clutch under an arm, dangle my legs over the window ledge and look down. I don't know which would be worse—falling to my embarrassing death or being caught out as a poopy fraud and humiliated in front of this posh family.

And—an embarrassing death it is!

I grasp the ivy with one hand, and although I have a firm grip, I don't know if I have the guts to fully commit to this mad plan. A loud knock on the bathroom door startles me and my heel slips, my clutch tumbles to the lawn below, and I swing out into mid-air with just one little hand grasping the ivy to prevent me from falling.

"Sal, everything all right in there?"

The sound of Sean's voice makes me panic even more. *What the fuck have I done?* As I swing slightly from side to side, I can make out Derek's passionate hand gestures through the window below me. "I'll be two seconds!" I manage to choke out.

I don't want to die, and the thought of Oscar being left on his own gives me the strength I need to reach for the sill with my free hand. Gaining a solid grip, I am now safely secured on the wall, where I get an inkling of how Spider-Man must feel. *C'mon Sal!* If I can save Clifford, I can save myself!

I muster up all the strength I have left and drag my body up and through the window. With a tremendous thud, I land on the bathroom floor and brush bits of ivy off my dress.

"Sal? What was that sound?"

"Just give me a minute!" I smooth my dress with my hands and spray Madeline's fancy air freshener, transporting myself briefly to the midst of a pine forest. I fling the door open, zip out, and tightly close it behind me so the stench doesn't flow out into the hallway where Sean is waiting.

"There you are. I thought you'd done a runner on me," Sean says with a low chuckle. He takes a step forward, but I swivel myself around to evade him.

"Nope. Thought about it though," I say with a slightly hysterical giggle. Sean smiles and gives me a look I haven't seen before. *Does he know I was up to no good?* I glide my hand toward the stairs. "Shall we?"

"Wait." His serious voice and smoldering eyes captivate me. "We did it. I mean, you did it. They approve!"

I gasp. "Are you serious? They approve of me!?"

"Dad's going to change the contract and have me as co-CEO. I'm so happy right now I could kiss you." He steps forward and I retreat again, getting perilously close to the top of the stairs.

Sean holds out a palm and grimaces. "Oh, I'm sorry. Please forgive me. I wasn't actually going to kiss you. Ha! Ew."

I try to ease the awkward tension. "Ah—no, it's just um ... that's great. I can't believe we did it!"

Seans eyes widen in alarm as my heel slips backwards off the top step. He quickly grabs me, stopping my fall. Both our gazes move to his hand, which has a firm grip on my arm. Fleetingly our eyes meet. The way he looks at me, gentle and kind, is enough to calm my racing heart from the shock of nearly suffering a *second* embarrassing death by undignified fall.

He clears his throat, "How about I go first? That way, if you fall, I'll catch you?"

I smile. "Sounds like a plan." I follow him to the bottom of the stairs and quickly retrieve my coat.

"Are you cold?"

"You know, I'm not feeling well," I respond nonchalantly, buttoning up my coat as fast as I can.

Sean twitches his nose. As he gets closer to me, he sniffs the air. "Can you smell that?"

I shake my head. "Nope."

He takes another step toward me.

"Don't come any closer!"

His eyes widen and mirth spreads over his face. "No!"

I huff out a breath, shrug my shoulders and whisper, "I *told you* I can't eat meat." Expecting him to be appalled I am slightly comforted by his hefty belly laugh, though it's a little too sexy for my liking.

"This isn't funny, Sean! Please, can we just go? You said it yourself—they've approved of me. Mission complete. Now get me out of here!" My words wash right over him as he indulges in more laughter.

Madeline strides into the hall with Clifford by her side. "What are you two giggling about?"

Clifford smiles, "I haven't seen you laugh like this in years."

Madeline swats at Clifford's arm. "Oh darling it's because he's in love!"

"Madeline, Clifford! Ha-ha, oh, he's just winding me up as usual." I playfully punch Sean's arm before making direct eye contact with Clifford. "How are you feeling?"

"Thanks to you, I'm alive." His eyes take in my coat. "You're not leaving already?"

Madeline perks up. "I should hope not. We haven't tried your cheesecake yet."

Sean throws an arm around me. "She's not feeling well, Mom. I think I better take her home."

I smile at Sean before I turn my attention to Madeline and Clifford. "I'm so sorry. It just came on suddenly. I don't want to put you at risk. I think you've been through enough for one night."

"How thoughtful of you, dear. Well, before you go, we wanted to say—" Madeline nudges Clifford's arm.

Clifford takes over. "We wanted to say *welcome to the family, Sally.*"

"Thank you, Clifford! I'm delighted to become part of it."

Madeline opens her arms, but I gracefully step back. "Oh, sorry, Madeline, I better stay away."

"Don't be silly. We're family now," Madeline hugs me tightly. Thankfully the hug is short-lived due to the interruption of Derek, making his presence known.

"Mom, Dad, aren't you forgetting something?" Derek stands behind Madeline with a phony grin on his face. Madeline struggles to speak, so Clifford takes the lead.

"Sean, Sally. Since you are getting married, we thought it would be a great idea if you moved the wedding forward to next weekend—prior to the announcement of our new co-CEOs."

My heart thumps to the floor. Suddenly, escaping down the ivy didn't seem like such a radical idea. It's as if a grenade has hit the room, and a flight or fight response is needed ASAP. Going by the fury on Sean's reddening face, he's going to choose fight.

Clifford proceeds, "I know this may seem sudden, but the timing couldn't be better. Son, this is an ideal opportunity that will redeem your reputation, and that in turn will benefit the company."

Madeline politely clears her throat. "What he *means* to say is this may be helpful, I know you're both too busy to organize a wedding. So why don't we take care of it for you? Sally, if Sean hasn't told you, we visit our lake house in Tahoe every Independence Day. It's the perfect setting!"

Sean and I bumble some awkward sounds that don't make sense.

Derek grins as he scrutinizes Sean. "What's the matter, little bro? I thought this is what you wanted?"

Sean's raging eyes bore back at him. "You put them up to this!"

As tensions heighten, I remember my goal to be in a relationship before I turn thirty. I know this isn't real, but the feeling of being accepted into an influential family of wealth has made me feel so important. It feels *great*. And I can't help but think that getting married on my birthday is a sign from the universe. While my brain has an indecisive game of ping-pong, my big fat mouth goes rogue and races away.

"We'll do it!"

Derek raises an eyebrow, and Madeline let out a sigh of happiness. Clifford nods like the deal is done, and Sean's head slowly turns to me.

"Sal," he says through gritted teeth.

"Madeline's right, honey! It makes sense. I need to focus on work and when you're CEO we won't have time to organize anything. If Madeline wants to plan the ceremony that would be absolutely splendid."

Madeline throws her arms around me, embracing me like I'm already part of the family. "I'm so happy! Independence Day it is!"

Madeline releases me and sniffs around the room. "Can anyone smell that?"

Sean places his hand on my back, guiding me swiftly to the front door. "Right, now that's settled, we'll be off."

"Yes, of you go, Sean. I have lots to do!"

Sean hovers in the doorway, "Mom."

"Yes, dear?"

"Small wedding, right? Just the family."

"Just the family."

"Thank you for a lovely dinner, everyone," I say while Sean propels me out the door, closing it before anyone can reply.

"Really Sally?"

I shrug my shoulders and open my palms. "You're welcome?"

His voice deepens. "Get in the car."

I can't tell if I'm afraid or slightly turned on. I should really respect his anger after what I've just accidentally agreed to, but why does he have to be so dominant and sexy when he's mad!

"Oh! Just one thing. I need to get my bag."

Sean shakes his head and groans. I stop him from opening the front door. "It's not in there!"

"Where is it, then?"

I curl up the corner of my mouth and squint my eyes. "Long story."

Chapter 13

Sal

MY EYES CUT AWAY from his thumb tapping on the steering wheel. "That went well," I say.

Sean doesn't even flinch an eyelid, focusing on the road ahead.

"I forgot how exhausting it is pretending to be someone else."

Sean lets out a breath that sounds like it has been trapped for hours. He pulls the Jeep off the road. "Have you lost your mind, Sally? Do you realize what you've just done?"

"Excuse me?! What *I've* just done? The nerve!" I cross my arms and stew in my anguish. We silently look out our respective windows until he turns his head to me.

"I'm sorry. I just didn't expect it to go like that. The wedding part, I mean."

"Me neither! Do you think I want to get married to a guy I've just met?" My exasperated tone makes him somber.

"You don't have to do this, you know," he says softly.

"I know. But this way, the deal is done. You'll get your grand title, and I'll get my twenty grand. Right?"

"I think I'll owe you a little more than that after a long weekend with my family."

"Your parents weren't as bad as I feared. Quite lovely, actually." I roll my eyes, "Derek, however."

Sean furrows his brow. "He knows something fishy is going on, I can feel it."

"How will we pull off three whole days with him around?" I ask.

"We'll just have to stick together until we say 'I do', I guess."

I nod, then part my lips, hesitant to say what I'm about to say. "Um, hate to bring it up. But since I'm your fiancée and all … what made your dad turn so dark on you last year?"

With a big groan he pulls out his phone and shows me an image of himself, clearly very drunk, putting one-hundred-dollar bills into a stripper's G-string while giving the thumbs up to the camera.

"Oh, I see," I say, pinching my lips together to trap my laughter.

"That's not even the funny part." He shows me another image that's been cropped to just show his face next to the stripper's bare butt, with text emblazoned across it:

Maxwell Gets Some Fresh Meat!

The laughter escapes, and I clap a hand over my mouth.

"Some funny guy thought it would be great to turn me into a meme, which went viral and was all over the company's socials. Now, Dad thinks I have a drinking problem. Hence not touching a drop in nearly eight months. I was celebrating my birthday, which to my regret got a bit out of hand. That's why he didn't want me to be the face of the company."

"I don't blame him," I say teasingly.

He tilts his head and twists one side of his mouth. "Whose side are you on, anyway?"

"Sorry, yours of course."

His shoulders relax, and his infectious smirky grin makes my belly tingle. "Thanks, Sal, for making things right again." He looks out the window and laughs, then mocks my attempt at playing a doctor.

"The oxygen in his brain will *fill up again,* then his vital signs *should* return to *normal.*"

I punch him playfully on the shoulder.

"Ow! What? It was brilliant!" he giggles, rubbing his arm. "But seriously, I don't know how you saved my dad, but you did. Thank you."

"Turns out you can learn a lot through watching TV and I've always wanted to play a character like a doctor, so I guess I got my wish. But if I'm going to pull this off, I'll need some new clothes."

"Done. Whatever you want. But what's wrong with the clothes you normally wear?"

"Trust me. My wardrobe is colorful, flowery, flirtatious, and what my friends would describe as provocative. I need to keep looking the part if you want this to work."

"You've got me intrigued now. I'm sure you'd look cute in anything."

I look out the car window to disguise the blush that blossoms across my face. Then I look back at him. "Oh, and one more thing." Sean narrows his eyes as I continue, "I'll need a wedding dress."

"Looks like I'm taking you shopping then." He starts the car and gives me a cheeky grin. "Let's get you home. I think someone needs a shower."

Oscar greets me at my front door, and when I see Carlos's eager face I can tell he's dying to know how it went.

"The tea, Sal, give it to me," Carlos demands.

I fuss over Oscar and walk to the kitchen.

Carlos strides up to me.

"Hello! How did it go? Did they approve?"

I pause, then smile. "Uh-huh."

"Yass bitch! I knew you'd pull it off! Did he give you the money?"

My lips twist and turn. "Not yet."

He steps back. "Whoa! Why not?"

I exhale and extend my hand. "There's one more thing I have to do first." His eyes widen and he swoons over my sparkly new ring.

"¡Dios mío! Chica, have you lost your mind?"

"Perhaps."

"*When?*"

"Next weekend."

He shakes his head, smiling from ear to ear. "Your life just got so interesting suddenly. This is way better than watching *Drag Race*. RuPaul, eat your heart out! Tell me *ev-ery-thing!*"

"I will. Right after I take a shower."

Waking up on Saturday morning to the sparkly ring on my finger is *the best way* to start the weekend. I'm not one for sleeping in, but I was awake all night thinking about Sean and what style of wedding dress I'll wear. My phone rings, breaking me out of my musing. I reach for it delicately, to avoid disturbing Oscar, who is fast asleep beside me.

"Morning, Piper."

"How was it? Please tell me he was worth standing us up for?"

"You could say that," I reply, glad she can't see the beaming smile on my face.

"Fran's coming around soon for brunch and bubbles—without the bubbles, of course! You in?"

I groan in response to her cheerful tone.

"You sound like you've just woken up."

"That's because I have."

"What are you still doing in—" Piper pauses and changes her tone, "Oh, I see. It went *really* well, didn't it?"

"No, Piper. I'm alone. Do you think I'd sleep with a guy after the first date?"

"I wouldn't judge you if you did! See you soon, then?"

"Fine, I'll get an Uber. See you soon."

My eyes glance over my ring as I press Piper's doorbell. *Ahh, fuck!* I quickly shove it in my bag just as Piper opens the door to greet me, wearing a sleek red summer dress. *"Oh my GOD!"* she cries.

I raise a hand to my lips. I have never received that kind of reaction from her before. "What's wrong?"

She pinches her thumb and forefinger together. "More like what's right!"

"Oh. Surprise!" I say, realizing she hasn't seen my new look.

"You look incredible! Come in. Fran has to see this."

I follow her down the pretty boutique-styled hallway and into the open kitchen, where Fran sits on a black leather stool eating a strawberry cupcake.

"Fran! Meet our new friend!" Piper exclaims.

Fran turns around before taking another bite, and her jaw drops to the floor. "Sal!?"

"Any cupcakes left for me?"

Fran gets up off her stool and inspects me. "Your hair. Your face. Your eyes!"

"I'm still getting used to it. I don't know if I like it."

"Girl, I love it! This is what I was talking about!"

"Thanks. I took your advice after all," I say, bouncing my hair with my hands.

"Woo-*wee!*" Fran says, returning to her stool.

"Sit down, Sal. I'll pour you a glass," Piper picks up a bottle of wine.

"Thanks, Piper." I sit next to Fran and she eyes me gleefully.

"No kids today, Fran?" I ask, receiving my rosé from Piper.

"They're having a day out with Jamal. I needed a break. Being a stay-at-home mom is not all it's cracked up to be. I'm exhausted!"

Piper laughs. "I don't blame you one bit, honey. That is why I don't have kids and never will! I don't know how you do it."

My eyes dance around, admiring the beautiful blush-toned room. "Gosh, I haven't been here in so long. Your place looks lovely, Piper."

"It helps when you're dating an interior designer."

Fran puts her hand on one hip. "Are you going to let Leo move in yet?"

"Calm down, Fran. It's only been four months. I'm still not sure."

I chime in. "Spoken by the girl who expects me to find a man in a month! I thought you said you'll know when you meet the right person?"

Piper screws up her face. "I did, didn't I?" Piper looks down in deep thought, then smiles at me. "Anyway, tell us how your date went last night!?"

I take a delicate sip of wine and lower the glass back to the counter, playing for time.

"Well, go on! You must like him if you changed your whole look for him," Fran exclaims.

I don't know how I will get out of this one. "Ooh! I've got some updates!" I say.

"Spit it!" Fran demands eagerly.

"You know how I caught my roommate Carlos wearing my lipstick?"

"Yeah," Fran replies, licking her icing.

"I know why. Get this! He wants to be a woman!"

Fran spits out her cupcake. "Wow! I did not see that one coming."

"Me neither. But now that I understand him better, he's really cool," I reply.

"You know what? It's very common these days. I remember we did an editorial for *Brides and Beauty* on this couple; one was a woman who transitioned into a man, and the other was a man who transitioned into a woman. It was one of our biggest features yet! Love is love!" Piper says, cleaning the crumbs off her glossy kitchen counter. One thing Piper hates is an unclean home. That's why Fran thinks Piper doesn't want Leo to move in, but I think it's because she secretly knows he's not the one.

"Good for him. Nowadays you can be whoever you want to be," Fran exclaims. "Sal, will you tell us how your date went, or was that another excuse so you could stay home in your fat pants?"

"For your information," I reach for a cupcake, "it went exceptionally well." I place some cupcake in my mouth and eat it with pleasure.

Fran smiles at Piper, and I prepare myself for an interrogation. "What's his name?" Fran asks.

I take my time to swallow, thinking about my response. Although acting is my chosen profession, I can't act my way out of a paper bag when it comes to Fran and Piper. They know me too well.

"Sean," I reply.

"Last name?" Fran asks.

I place my finger to my lips. "Ah, I think it was ... Maaa ... Max ..."

"Maxwell?" Piper suggests.

"Hmm, yes, Maxwell. That's it."

Fran whips out her phone, and I know she's getting her google on. "Fran, what are you doing?"

"What? I'm just making sure he's real."

"Of course he's real. Why would I make this up?"

"I know *you're* not making it up. I want to see if he's good enough for my homegirl." I exhale, seeing her mischievous face light up. She places her phone on the kitchen island.

"And yes, yes he is!"

Piper grabs the phone, and the image on the screen is of Sean dressed like a cowboy, holding a clipboard. "Is that him, Sal?" Piper asks.

Slowly, I nod.

"Holy heck Sal, he's bloody beautiful," Piper says with twinkling eyes.

"Did you read the part about his millionaire family!?" Fran asks.

Piper's eyes scroll down the phone. "Wow, Maxwell's Meat, huh? I didn't think you'd go for that, Sal?"

"Who says a vegetarian and a meat-eater can't be together?" I reply.

Piper hums. "True! What's he like?"

"To be honest, he initially seemed like another LA asshole. But once I got to know him"—I smile, remembering him saving me from falling down the stairs—"he's amazing."

Fran and Piper look at each other like they have just won a chess game.

"Where did you meet?" Fran asks.

My confident tone drops. "At Happy Day Groceries."

Fran lets out a roaring laugh. "Did you both reach for the same banana and accidentally touch hands like in the movies?"

"Not exactly," I say, shifting my gaze from side to side. "I work there now."

"Aw, Sal. You got a new job?" Piper puts her hand on her heart.

"Beggars can't be choosers, right? It's only until I find something better."

"No, Sal, that's great. I'm proud of you." Piper leans over and gives me a pity-pat that grinds my teeth.

"Hell! Get a ring on that finger pronto, girlfriend! Then you'll be able to quit in no time!" Fran exclaims jokingly.

I don't know how to react to such an eerily accurate sentiment. I laugh in an over-the-top manner that's so contagious Fran and Piper join in too. I use this giggly moment to casually reach for my bag and place it in my lap.

Fran's laugh fades. "Going somewhere?"

"Nope," I say.

"What's with the bag?"

"Fran, you know I like having my bag near me at all times."

Fran squints her eyes and studies my face. "Hmm. I know that look. It's the look you make when you're hiding something. Either that or you're anxious, and I know you're not anxious. Piper, back me up here."

"Fran, leave her alone."

Fran and I lock eyes in a staring competition. I break contact first and look down at my bag. *Shit!*

"What's in there, Sal?"

"Nothing, Fran!"

"Then you won't mind me taking a look." Fran swoops the bag right out of my lap and takes it to the corner of the kitchen.

"What are you doing?" I try to reach for it, but Fran uses her height against me.

"Fran! Are you nuts? Give Sal her bag back!"

"Right after I take a little peek." Fran turns her back to me, and I silently rage as she rummages through it. Then Fran slowly twists to face me. The horror on her face makes me think she's seen the ring, and my anxiety kicks in.

"I'm so sorry, Sal. I don't know what came over me."

Fran's apologetic tone grants me some relief, my secret is still safe. But my too-quick retrieval of the bag flings it into the air and it tumbles as it falls, landing on Piper's feet. I scramble to the granite floor to pick up makeup, loose change, receipts, but the ring is nowhere to be found.

Fran joins me, "Here, I'll help."

"No, Fran! You've done enough!" I stand up and glower around the kitchen. "Where is it?"

"Where's what?" Fran asks, struggling to get off her knees.

With a gentle tone, Piper quietly speaks. "Is this what you're looking for, Sal?"

My head sharply turns to Piper, whose eyes shine at the sight of the ring she holds in her porcelain hand. I regain composure and calmly take the ring from her. I slide it onto my finger and sit back down, sipping my wine like nothing ever happened.

I coolly observe their bewildered faces. I cough. "Is it dusty in here, or is it just me?"

Piper frantically scans the kitchen. "Dust?!"

"Relax, Piper. There's no dust." Fran turns to me. "I knew it!"

"Is this true, Sal? You're getting married?" Piper says with concern, but her eyes are busy inspecting every surface.

My upright posture slumps, and I nod.

"What! When?" Piper asks.

"On my birthday," I reply, knowing I'm in for a grand old lecture.

"What! That's *next weekend!*" Fran says, her voice rising in volume.

"Surprise! Meeting someone before I turn thirty is easy after all. Yay me!"

"Have you lost your mind? This is next-level crazy!" Fran exclaims.

"Sure I've only known him for one night, but you said it, Piper—when you know, you know. Your parents were engaged after six weeks."

"And look what happened to them! Also there's a huge difference between six weeks and one night Sal. I mean, with everything going on in your life, I didn't think—"

I cut Piper off like a sharp knife. "Didn't think what? That someone like Sean could love a mess like me? That no one would ever take me seriously?" I huff. "You know what, no one *has* ever taken me seriously, now for once in my life someone *is*, and I'm going to roll with it!"

Fran adds her two cents. "Look, he's cute and rich. I'll give you that. But what if he's a murderer, a wife-beater, or a cheater? You didn't even know his last name! You've made some questionable choices in your life Sal, but this is beyond ridiculous. Your parents will *FREAK!*"

"They're not going to find out," I say, crossing my arms.

"I know you thought you would end up with someone before you're thirty, but I can't support you on this. It's insane!" Piper exclaims.

My lip starts to wobble, I know they're right. "I knew you would disapprove. That's why I didn't want you to know. You could have just been happy for me. I'm not going to be Single Sal anymore!" I throw my bag over my shoulder, swig back the last of my wine and storm out of the room.

As I charge down Piper's hallway I hear her call out, "Sal! Where are you going?"

Chapter 14

Sal

"**S**OMEONE SEEMS HAPPY TODAY," Carlos says, slurping down his cereal while he scrutinizes me as though he's watching a spy movie.

"Well *yeah*, I'm going shopping!" I reply from where I stand at the living room window dressed in a pink and yellow body-con dress.

"Someone will have to look after Oscar while you're away next weekend."

I turn my attention from the window to Carlos and pout my lips. "Would you?"

"Sure. I was just waiting for you to ask."

"Sorry, I've had a lot on my mind."

"You've certainly got some*one* on your mind," he murmurs.

Endorphins zap through my body at the sight of my phone lighting up with a message from Sean. "He's here!"

"Be careful, chica. He doesn't have the best reputation, and he's using you."

"No, *I* am using *him*," I say defiantly. But I receive the warning loud and clear. However, I hope my sensitive heart heard it too. I wipe my damp palms on my dress, and with a quick salute to Carlos, I'm out the door.

"Rodeo Drive!" I exclaim excitedly as we drive down the iconic street lined with palm trees and nice cars everywhere I look. The sight of luxe stores like Yves Saint Laurent and Fendi makes me salivate. My usual shopping routine consists of thrift stores and online bargains.

My starry eyes beam, and when Sean looks at me, his dimples crease. "You said you wanted to look the part." He pulls into a parking space, and exhales dramatically. "Come on. Let's get this over and done with. Shopping bores the hell out of me."

I clap my hands together like a giddy schoolgirl.

Tailored suits, designer handbags and Rolex watches beckon to us as we stroll the cobblestone pavement and take in the European charm. I stop at the sight of a seafoam silk cocktail dress in the Gucci store window. Sean sees my gleaming eyes and tilts his head toward the door. "Come on, let's go in here."

"Really?"

"Really. Just don't get too carried away. We're only together three days."

Side by side we enter the prestigious two-story store with its ruby-red walls framing glass cabinets that hold glamorous bags, hats, and accessories. Fashionistas browse through racks of high-end items that are lined up near the large window where the dress calls my name.

A redheaded woman approaches us, but I can tell she only really sees Sean. Her polished appearance makes me second-guess my outfit, and I worry she can sense an outsider in her midst.

"Good morning. Can I help you with anything today, sir?"

"Yes. The green dress in the window. Can she try it on, please?"

The woman briefly looks at me, then back at Sean. "Is this your sister?"

"No. Fiancée." He puts his arm around me, and instantly I feel protected against any judgment coming my way.

With a halfhearted smile the woman replies, "Excellent choice. I'll hang it in the dressing room for you. Will that be all, sir?"

"No, we'll keep looking. Thank you."

I give Sean a look of gratitude, still comfortably under his arm.

"Well, what are you waiting for?" He releases me, and I prowl the clothing racks like a child in a candy store.

After carefully choosing suitable outfits for the weekend, which include a ruffled chiffon shirt, a red polo dress, a floral-print maxi dress, and a vintage-style blazer, I make my way to the changing room.

Sean

I wait outside the changing room with my chin dipped toward my feet, which are tapping lightly on the antique rug. "Are you ready yet, Sal?"

"Yup! I've just got one more to try on," she calls.

My eyes catch a glimpse of her calf through the curtain. I force myself to look away, but I can't resist. I look back. My eyes travel up her leg as far as the curtain will allow, and I spring out of my seat to stop myself. I cough to cover my discomfort and try to pull myself together.

"You okay, Sean?" Sal asks through the curtain.

"I'm good," I reply with a weak voice.

Sal brushes through the curtain, and I stare at her as if I've never seen her before.

"You like?" she asks.

I take in her alluring body, lingering at the V-shaped neckline where her cleavage is perfectly displayed. I don't know much about fashion, but the braided waist accentuates her petite curves, and the ruffly-looking sleeves radiate sophistication. *Why can't I stop looking at her?* My mind is drifting and I no longer feel in control. *Shit!*

"You don't like it? I knew it was a little too much …"

Quick, say something, you idiot! "No. You look gorgeous. It's perfect."

"Oh. Thank you. Are you sure you want to get all these?" She lowers her voice, "I mean, look at the price tags! And we haven't even got the wedding dress yet."

Oh fuck! I look at my watch. "About that."

"Yeah?"

"There's been a change of plans."

"We're not getting married?"

I chuckle at the absurdity of it all.

"No, we are," I reply, strangely elated at the note of disappointment in her voice. "Mom wants to see you."

"Madeline does? Why?"

"You'll see."

Sal

I'm *so* glad I changed into the floral Gucci dress now that I'm sitting in front of Madeline at her dining table. Together with Sean, we browse wedding planner books and brochures while tasting decadent cake samples.

"Which one do you like dear? Vanilla, butterscotch, or lemon cream? I love the butterscotch!" Madeline says.

"They're all so wonderful." I turn to Sean. "What do you think, darling?"

"Whatever you decide is what we'll have. Happy wife, happy life, right?" He excuses himself from the table. "I'll leave you two to it."

"Butterscotch it is, Madeline!" I exclaim.

"I'm glad you agree," Madeline replies. She holds up a menu. "I think this selection will be sure to delight our guests."

I put my cake fork down and read the thick card.

Appetizer – grilled salmon with
a caramelized scallop, fennel and citrus

Entrée – molasses-glazed eye fillet,
heirloom carrots and pomegranate jus

Dessert – vanilla bean crème brûlée
with basil emulsion.

I raise my eyebrows, impressed. "It sounds superb!"

"Great. Now, what about your hair and makeup?"

"Oh! I know someone who can do that for me. I'll ask him."

"Marvelous. I've hired help to assist with everything else. There's just one important thing missing."

I'm perplexed. "Oh?"

"Come with me," Madeline says, and I follow her up the staircase.

Sean

I tap on Dad's office door, pushing it open to see him behind his large oak desk.

"Hey, Dad. You busy?"

He peers at me through his reading glasses. "I take it you've chosen a cake?"

"I thought I'd leave all that up to the girls. I've got more important things to worry about."

"What could be more important than your wedding, son?"

"I wanted to talk to you about the contract."

Dad leans back in his chair. "No need. It's all sorted. Our lawyers are getting the contracts ready for you and Derek to sign. I thought we'd do that the day after the wedding when we get back from the lake. You will sign on as co-CEO with Derek and share joint responsibilities."

"Sounds great. Thank you." I squint my eyes and gather my courage. "Will we get paid the same?"

"Yes, Sean," he replies with a raised eyebrow.

My shoulders drop, and I feel my face soften with relief. "How did Derek feel about that?"

"He'll get over it."

"Thanks, Dad. I won't let you down. I better get back to Sal. Who knows what Mom is making her agree to."

As I reach the doorway, Dad clears his throat, "Sean."

"Yeah?"

"You did well. We like her. Forgive me son, but at first, I thought she was a ploy to leverage your way into the CEO position. But after seeing you two together, I can tell she's the real deal. I see you're ready to be the man I always thought you would be."

My heart sinks into the abyss of my chest. My carefree face starts to tense up with guilt.

"Thanks, Dad."

Sal

Puffs, lace, frills, and a time-warp to the seventies are all I see when I look at my reflection in the standing mirror beside Madeline's king-size bed.

"What do you think, Sally?" Madeline asks.

I gulp and conjure up a smile. "I don't know what to say."

"Say you'll wear it."

I turn away from the mirror and sit at the end of the bed, wiping a tear from my cheek.

Madeline rushes to my side. "What's the matter, dear?"

"I always thought my mom and best friends would be with me to choose a dress."

Madeline's voice eases, "Oh, of course. I'm sorry. I was just trying to help. I've always wanted a daughter to wear my wedding dress. Victoria was the wrong size, but it fits you perfectly."

I can't bring myself to speak. Everything is getting way too real.

"Have you chosen your bridesmaid's dresses yet?"

"They can't make it."

"Oh? And your parents?"

"They can't make it at such short notice either."

Madeline pushes her fingers into her temple. "Oh dear, maybe we did rush this along. Perhaps we should reschedule so all your family and friends can be there?"

"No! I mean, no thank you. You've gone to so much trouble already, and you're right. Sean and I just don't have the time to organize a wedding right now. You're doing us *such* a favor." I stop wallowing in my sorrow and remind myself this isn't real.

"You'll meet my family soon enough," I say, bouncing off the bed and twirling around. "I'll wear the dress. I love it!"

Sal

No words are spoken during the drive back to my apartment, where we sit in the carpark drowning in the dismal energy that swamps us.

"Thanks for agreeing to wear Mom's dress. It made her day. Her life even."

I turn my head slightly in his direction. "She did look happy, didn't she?" I sigh. "Sean, what will she think when this is all over?"

"She'll bounce back. I won't announce our breakup until months after the wedding. You're free to do what you want once the contracts are signed."

I wish it were that easy. I look down at my fake ring and frown.

"The rest is up to me to handle, Sal," Sean says, tilting my chin toward him with his hand. "It'll be okay, don't worry."

The energy suddenly starts to sizzle. The car heats up, and tiny tingles spread from my face down my spine. I have to remind my heart to protect itself from men like Sean before I do something I'll regret. I pull away and say, "Thanks for today. I had fun."

"Yeah, me too. Who knew I'd have fun shopping?"

I smile and retrieve my bags from the back seat. "Thanks for the clothes, Sean."

"You're welcome. I'll pick you up first thing Friday morning?"

I flash him a quick smile before walking toward my building. I try to refrain from looking back at him, but when I do he's staring at me with smoldering eyes and that delicious smirk, and I feel myself go weak.

Chapter 15

Sal

THE WEEK FLIES BY in a blur, and suddenly Thursday morning arrives. Between work and perfecting my new style and authoritative persona for the biggest role of my life, I am too busy to think about my growing feelings for Sean.

There's still no word from Fran or Piper, just a couple of missed calls from my mom. But that's how I like it. Well, until this wedding is over anyway. No one will ruin my big fat fake wedding or my big fat real paycheck!

I miss girl talk with Fran and Piper, but I have found a new friendship in Carlos, who has supported me when imposter syndrome visits. I admire his courage to finally be who he wants without caring what people think of him. He owns who he is, and it's refreshing. Especially in the acting world, where everyone I know will happily change themselves to get ahead. Myself included, I guess. I have spent my whole life trying to please people, only to feel confused about who I truly am.

Carlos is excited to do my glam for the wedding. To show my appreciation, I give him some clothes that I loved when I was twenty-five, but now seem skimpy af. If they help Carlos express who he is, who am I to judge?

I walk into work on my last day as a broke, single woman and join the team meeting that takes place every morning before the store opens.

Helga stands in front of everyone like an angry teacher about to assign homework. "Right, this won't take long as we have a busy day ahead. Every man and his wife will be in here today buying food for the long weekend. I want you all on your game and looking happy, even if you're not. Got it!?"

Everyone nods like lifeless robots in agreement.

"If you need motivation, look to Sally. She's been here a measly two weeks and already shows signs of getting staff member of the month. Well done, Sally."

"Thank you, Helga," I reply with delight.

"Excuse me, Helga! Who got staff member of *last* month?" Jeremy asks, raising his hand.

"No one! You're all sad little sausages that look depressed to be here." Helga claps her hands. "We're called Happy Day Groceries for a reason, people! If you want to know why Sally is in the running for staff member of the month, it is because she knows how to smile and make our customers feel special. Revenue has dropped ten percent against last year, so we need to sell, sell, sell!"

Murmurs and groans filter the room. "Quiet! As you are aware, we have been promoting Maxwell's Meat this month, and the company director is visiting us today to look at how we are showcasing their brand."

My eyes pop, and my jaw drops. "*What?* The Maxwells are coming here?"

"Yes. Derek and Victoria Maxwell. So, we are all to be on our best behavior. No slacking off!" Helga eyeballs Jeremy. "Jeremy, Tommy's away sick today, so you'll be in the sausage suit."

"Ah, man! Really, Helga?"

Helga mimics his dreary tone. "Really, Jeremy."

"I'll do it!" I exclaim.

Everyone stares at me like I'm out of my mind. No one ever wants to do that job.

"No, Sally. I need your bright and bubbly smile on checkout. You're good for business."

"It's no problem. It isn't that bad! I *am* the new girl, and I haven't paid my dues yet."

Helga observes Jeremy's hopeful face. "Please, Helga, that suit makes my face break out," he begs.

"Look, we have no time for this. Fine! Sally, suit up and hand out as many flyers as you can. Especially when you see two suits come near you."

"Got it, Helga," I say, saluting her.

"Alright, everyone, put those smiles on and go to your stations."

While everyone disperses, Jeremy approaches me. "Thanks, Sal, you're awesome."

"Don't sweat it. We can't have you breaking out, can we."

I stand in front of Happy Day Groceries, ruminating on how absurd it is that I'm *happy* to be back in this hideous sausage suit. There is no way Derek will ever get to see my face.

Hours go by as I hand out flyers in the scorching heat. I purposely skip my break, but wish I hadn't as fatigue creeps in. But I'm determined to stay in this suit until I know Derek has come and gone.

No customers are around, so I don't think it will hurt to rest my legs on a park bench next to the store. My mouth is dry, and my head is spinning. My body gravitates along the bench where I rest my head and let my eyes close for a moment. When I open them, I can just make out a pair of black leather shoes through my tiny peepholes.

"What is this!?"

I recognize Derek's voice and struggle to a standing position where I can see his angry face and his wife, Victoria, shaking her pixie-cut styled head.

"What are you doing sitting down when you should be working? You're representing *my* brand, buddy!" Derek barks.

"This is unacceptable," Victoria says, writing a note on her clipboard.

"You're damn right it's unacceptable!"

"No darling, I mean the suit." Victoria takes a closer look and observes every detail including the peepholes, through which she appears to stare directly into my eyes. It's all over now. I wish and pray for a UFO to come down from the sky and abduct me.

"Well! What do you have to say for yourself?" Derek growls.

My dry mouth and froggy throat stop me from saying a word.

"Darling, give him a break. His life must be terrible if his job is to live in this horrid sausage all day. Which looks more like a giant poop, don't you think?"

"His life's about to get worse after I speak to his manager."

I muster up the deepest, manliest voice I can. "Sorry, sir."

"You will be." He storms off, and Victoria follows him with her lips pressed tightly together.

I go back to my original position. After another grueling hour handing out flyers, I see Derek and Victoria exit the store. I get as close to them as possible so they can see me making an energetic effort to entice customers to receive a flyer. I think Derek is about to grill me again, but he stops a few feet away.

"Darling, it's just a small drop in revenue. We'll have to go back to the drawing board and develop some fresh marketing ideas. Maybe Sean joining you will be a good thing," Victoria is saying.

"Ha! He doesn't know it yet, but he is not joining me as CEO. I'm telling you, Vic, something is wrong with his new fiancée, and I'm going to find out what it is. I can't even find her on social media." He looks across at me, and I pretend I wasn't listening. "Come on, let's get out of here. This place is a dump."

I entertain some nearby children, and he approaches me on his way to his car.

"You're lucky you weren't fired for your unprofessional behavior today, Mister. If I see you slacking off again, I'll make it my business to fire you myself. Do you understand?"

I nod, but as soon as I see them drive off I throw the last of the flyers in the trash. Then I rush to Helga's office and tear the suit off like an angry bear. I collapse to the floor gasping for air. That's when I hear Helga's finger tapping on her desk. I glare up at her, she's giving me an exasperated frown.

I toss and turn in my sleep, having night terrors where I'm being chased by Derek wearing a sausage suit. When daylight strikes, I race out of bed and spend the morning making myself feel pretty for my trip to the lake. I think the cream chiffon shirt with a pair of jeans is a classy but casual choice.

I roll my pink hard-shell suitcase out to the living room, strike a pose with an imaginary mic and belt, "Here comes the bride, all dressed in white, mascara running down her—" *Wait—what are the words? Shoot! Did I pack my waterproof mascara!?*

After I'm certain I'm armed with the makeup and clothes I need, I go to the kitchen and rummage around in the pantry. Carlos glides out of his room and sizes me up.

"Chica, if I didn't know any better, I'd think you're catching feelings for this guy," he says teasingly.

"Me? Ha! Just because I'm singing. Besides, why would he be interested in me? I have nothing to offer but a fake mar-riage"—I pull out a can of beans—"and some expired food!" I throw the beans in the trash and open a fresh can of dog food for Oscar.

My face lights up as I hear my phone chime. Then I frown, glancing at the caller ID.

"Aren't you going to get that?" Carlos asks.

"It's Mom. She can't find out about this."

"Isn't it best to speak to her now, or she'll just keep calling you over the weekend."

I nod, putting the phone to my ear. "Hi, Mom!"

"Sweetie, I've been calling you all week. I was worried."

"Sorry, Mom. I've been so busy with my new job."

"A new job? Amazing! Where?"

"Please don't judge, but I'm a checkout girl at Happy Day Groceries."

"What! What happened to your teaching job?"

"It's a long story. I don't want to talk about it right now."

"Well, I rang to see if you still want me to arrange a birthday party. It's only three days away, so I need to know."

"Oh, shoot, I forgot about that. I don't want any fuss. It's just another day. But thank you."

"You only turn thirty once, sweetie. We have to do something."

"I can't. I'm going away this weekend."

"Oh! Where?"

"Tahoe."

"With the girls?"

"No," I pause. "With another friend."

"I see. It's that boy you went on a date with a while ago, isn't it?"

I squint my eyes and remember Ronnie. I hate lying to my mom, but I'm in too deep now. I grin and play along. "Um. Yes, actually. Him."

"I'm so pleased to see you putting yourself out there again! Make sure you put your best foot forward. Your ovaries aren't getting any younger."

I hear a honk from outside. I rush to the window and see Sean looking up at me with his cheeky smirk.

"Mom, I gotta go! Love you."

"Have fun, Sal. Be safe."

I put my phone in my bag and flutter my hands before grabbing my suitcase. "Okay, I'll text you the address. Remember, Monday morning. Don't be late. And don't tell anyone!"

"Hand on heart, I won't," Carlos promises, opening the front door for me.

"Oh, and don't forget Oscar gets fed twice a day."

"Yes, yes, get out of here already!" he says, shooing me along.

I squeal excitedly and skip out the door.

Sean's leaning on his car. He's wearing blue jeans, and a white T-shirt that accentuates his muscular physique. A baseball cap matches his blue eyes, and I can't help reflecting on how much sexier his casual look is than his fancy-dancy business suit.

He opens the trunk of his car before surprising me with a hug. I didn't expect it, but once in his arms, I feel safe. He smells like a masculine feast of goodness. As I nestle into his shoulder, I feel his breath on my neck. Conflicting emotions and lust swirl inside me like a storm that leaves me feeling sick. I pull away and smile at him. "Let's do this."

He responds with a smile and throws my suitcase into the Jeep. "You do realize that once you hop in this car, there's no going back. This is your last chance to run away while you still can," he says.

"I'm *in it* to *win it* now. Besides, I had nothing better to do this weekend."

He raises an eyebrow and tilts his head. "Liar."

Chapter 16

Sal

AFTER AN ENTERTAINING SEVEN-HOUR drive, I feel armed with the confidence I need to play Sean's fiancée. We spent the time getting to know each other better, and I was comforted by his genuine desire to learn more about me. No man has ever asked me questions beyond what kind of underwear I wear.

Sean turns down the volume on Johnny Cash, foiling my attempts to get him to sing along. "Are you always this weird?" he asks.

"Yup!" I finish my air-drum solo with a flourish and grin at him.

He shakes his head and chuckles.

The whole trip I've wanted to divulge what I overheard Derek say. However, I don't want to dampen his cheerful mood or add pressure on such an important weekend. The best thing I can do is bring my A-game.

"So, I know you're a workaholic, and you like to watch the discovery channel. But who are you when you're not working with the animals?" I ask.

He smirks. "You still want to know more about me, huh?"

"Yeah. I do."

"Well, what you see is what you get. I don't like to play games. Contrary to what you might have read on the internet."

"I may have seen you being referred to as ... a womanizer."

"Ha! And that is why I stay off my phone as much as possible. I don't understand why someone wants to write about me. I'm a ranch manager. I'm not that interesting."

"Hmm, that's debatable. Have you always worked for your dad?"

"Ever since I was old enough to drive. I haven't thought much about other career avenues." His tone lowers. "Well, when I was younger, I did want to be a photographer. But there was no way my parents would allow that."

"Why not?"

He smiles and shakes his head. "You don't know my parents. For some reason, they think all artists are poor, struggling, second-class citizens." He sighs. "Besides, I always thought I'd take over the company one day. I just didn't know I would have to fight so hard for it." He shakes his head. "Eighteen years of loyalty to my dad washed away because of a damn *meme*. Go figure that one out."

I throw him a sympathetic look before glancing past him out the window, where I see a sign welcoming us to South Lake Tahoe.

"We're here?!" I exclaim.

"We sure are," he confirms proudly, driving past rocky mountains, native pine trees, lake views, and beautiful cabins. Within a few minutes, we roll up a driveway through tall spiky trees that thin out to reveal a lavish two-story chalet-style home—a home where I could happily spend three days away from the concrete jungle. Sean parks at the back of the house.

"Come on. I'm sure Victoria is dying to meet you," he says with disdain.

I grab his hand before he leaves the car. "Sean."

He looks down at my hand. "Yeah?"

"Your brother. I think you were right about him—he knows something fishy is going on."

He cups his hand over mine. "Stick close to me, and you'll be fine."

Sean retrieves his luggage, and my suddenly-hungry eyes fixate on his big flexing muscles. Mm yummy—*For the love of ice cream Sal, get yourself together!*

"Uh, Sal. You all good?" he asks.

"Yeah! It's so hot is all." *So, so hot.*

He answers with a grin while picking up my suitcase.

"Sean, I'll take mine."

"No, I got it." He passes me a small cooler instead, "You can bring this if you like." I take the cooler, which is heavier than I expected.

"What's in here?"

He winks. "It's a surprise."

Sean opens the back door and calls to see if anyone is home, and I catch a glimpse of lawn sloping toward the lake. "Come on, they're probably around the front," Sean says, leading me inside.

He leaves our luggage in the rustic living room, where a stone fireplace takes center stage and the high ceilings feature old wooden beams that match the polished floors. He drops the cooler off in the kitchen and grabs my hand. We follow the sound of classical music onto a wide deck that overlooks lush green lawn stretching down to the lakefront, where several jet skis float by a dock.

Madeline, Clifford, Derek, and his wife Victoria sit around an impressive cheeseboard, drinking wine. Their chatter abruptly stops. All eyes are on me.

"Here's the bride and groom to be!" Madeline exclaims, rising from her chair. She welcomes us with a hug and a kiss, followed by Clifford, who seems a lot more relaxed than he did at the dinner from hell.

"I called out, but no one heard me," Sean says.

"I'm sorry, dear. We were having too much fun! Sally, darling, you know Derek." Derek doesn't bother getting out of his chair but makes a pathetic attempt to raise his glass.

Madeline sweeps her hand in Victoria's direction. "And this is my wonderful daughter-in-law, Victoria."

"Oh, stop it, Madeline," Victoria says. She reaches out her hand and gives me a flimsy handshake. Victoria seems like a woman that will take a while to warm up to. Her cold stare and lukewarm smile spike uneasy prickles down my back.

While the men congregate, I gracefully accept a glass of wine from Madeline and remind myself not to drink too much in case I reveal more than I should. I admire the sun melting over the glistening lake before I sit next to Victoria.

"Stunning, isn't it?" Madeline asks.

"Totally breathtaking."

Victoria crosses her legs and hovers her glass of wine in the air. "So, Derek tells me you're a doctor, Sally? It must be horrible prodding at sick bodies all day?"

I clear my throat and swallow the urge to laugh in her cold face. "Yes. I am. I love helping people, and everyone needs a doctor right? Even you!"

"Only sick people need doctors. I haven't been to a doctor, dentist or therapist in years," Victoria says flashing me a smug smile.

"Lucky you then!" I look to Madeline, who's smiling at me proudly.

Victoria puts her glass down and crosses her arms. "I'd imagine living in LA is a lot different from New York."

"I'm used to it. I grew up in Santa Monica, that's where my parents live, so I know my way around."

"That's right. Derek told me you met Sean at a grocery store of all places," Victoria tilts her head back and laughs. "Not exactly romantic!"

"You can find love anywhere these days."

A little girl who looks around six years old leaps into Sean's arms, catching my attention. "Katie-pie! How's my favorite niece?"

"I'm good, Uncle Sean."

"Were you picking daisies?"

Katie nods.

"For me?" Katie shakes her head and looks over at me.

Victoria summons Katie with her hands. "Katie, honey, come meet Sally."

Sean releases Katie, and she tentatively walks toward me with some hand-picked daisies in her fist. I crouch down to make her feel at ease. "You must be Katie?" Katie nods, giving me the daisies. "Ooh, thank you so much, Katie!"

Her rosy cheeks beam. "You're pretty."

I put my hand to my heart. "Thank you!" I whisper. "Not as pretty as you."

Katie giggles, looking at me in wonder. "You're not fake. You're real!"

I don't know how to react to her comment. I laugh it off, hoping everyone else will too.

"Katie, where on earth did you get that idea from?" Madeline asks.

Katie hesitates before looking at Madeline. "Daddy told Mommy he thinks Sally's fake."

Derek rises from his chair. "Katie!"

Victoria gasps and gives Derek a look of concern.

"Oh, did he now?" I smile at Sean, who puts his arm around my waist while addressing Katie.

"Katie. Does Sally look fake to you?"

"Nope! Kiss her, kiss her!"

"Katie, don't be rude," Victoria bellows.

"That's okay, Victoria. I know what kids can be like." I give Sean a quick peck on the cheek, "There!"

Derek laughs. "What are we, in a Disney movie?"

Before I can react, Sean pulls me in and squeezes me against his chest. He kisses me with his soft lips—invisible electricity sparks between us. Heat pierces my cheeks as I melt into his body. Time stops, then so does the kiss, leaving a parade of warm fuzzy feelings in the depth of my stomach. I'm embarrassed I let myself get carried away in front of everyone. Our gaze intensifies, then the silence is broken by Katie.

"Eww—yucky! That was *not* like Frozen, Mommy."

Our undeniable attraction causes everyone to shut their mouths.

"Everyone happy now?" Sean asks in a firm tone. My eyes flicker to Derek, but he ignores any eye contact.

"Great, I'll take the silence as a yes!" Sean exclaims, brushing his hands against each other.

Two hours pass and the cicadas and crickets hum their tunes among the tall, dark trees. A yawn escapes me, and I see Katie nestle her head into Victoria's chest. "Mommy, I'm tired."

"Let's get you to bed," Victoria replies before excusing her-self.

Sean sets his glass of water down and darts a look at me. "Sal, it's been a long day. I'll show you to our room."

"Our room? I don't mind sleeping in a separate room."

"Nonsense Sally, if you're old enough to get married, you're old enough to sleep in the same bed. I remember what it was like just before we were married, right Clifford?"

Clifford raises an eyebrow, twirling the stem of his port glass.

"We couldn't keep our hands off each other!" Madeline recalls.

"Okay, Mom, that's our cue to go. I'll see you in the morn-ing," he kisses her on the cheek and gives an affable nod to Clifford and Derek.

I stand up and join Sean. "Goodnight, all. See you in the morning."

I shadow Sean as he carries our luggage down a long hallway decorated with family portraits. He points to the first door on the right. "That's my parent's bedroom, but Mom sleeps in this room," he says, pointing to the door opposite. A few steps further he opens the door to a large bedroom with a fireplace and an ensuite. A couch is positioned under a wide window displaying panoramic views of the lake.

"What do you think?"

I drop my handbag and run straight to the window. "I think I could live here forever." My eyes bounce around the room, landing on a huge framed photograph of a black bear. "*Eek*, oh my gosh!"

Sean chuckles. "Don't worry. It's not going to bite you. I took that last summer."

I take a closer look. "You took this?"

He nods. "Took me a while to get the money shot while trying not to piss myself, but yeah."

"Wow. It's beautiful."

"Thanks, it's a hobby that keeps me sane."

I fidget my hands and look at the bed. We both stand still as if unsure of what to say next. Sean rubs his thighs, then clasps his hands together. "You take the bed. I'll have the couch."

"Oh, thank you."

We share a moment full of lingering emotions from our earlier kiss. Neither of us chooses to bring it up. Sean takes some sleepwear from his luggage and goes into the ensuite. "I'll give you your space."

I bobble up and down on the king-size bed then lay back like a luxuriant starfish. *I could get used to this.*

Sean

My eyes spring open to the most annoying alarm I have ever heard. I peer over at Sal on the bed, oblivious to the jarring noise. I follow the screeching across the room and tentatively reach into her bag, where I locate her phone. I turn the alarm off. While I'm holding the phone, a Snapchat notification from a guy named Zac flashes on her screen. I didn't think to ask if she was seeing anyone.

I'm deciding if I should feel concerned when Sal rises from her sleep abruptly and sees me still holding her phone. I raise my palms in the air in a calming gesture.

"What are you doing with my phone?"

Slowly, I lower the phone and slip it back into her bag. "Nothing. I wasn't snooping, I promise. I just turned off your outrageously annoying alarm."

Sal's eyes dance around the room and crash-land on my bare chest. "Oh," she says, noticing her clothes. "I fell asleep, didn't I?"

"Sure did," I reply.

"Did you take my shoes off?" Sal asks.

I hope she doesn't think I'm a creep. "I just wanted you to sleep comfortably, that's all."

"Oh, thank you. That's … sweet."

I grab a towel already placed in the room by Mom and throw it at her. "Get up. I'm taking you out."

"Where are we going?"

"It's a surprise. I just hope there's some comfortable clothes and shoes in that gigantic suitcase of yours."

Chapter 17

Sal

Hand in hand, Sean and I glide into the kitchen area, looking like we're going to the gym. Madeline pours freshly brewed coffee at the dining table, where there is a delicious-looking array of croissants, fruit, and muesli. Victoria helps Katie spread raspberry jam on her toast while Derek and Clifford make small talk about finance.

"Morning, everyone!" I say, approaching the table.

"Morning dear, sleep well?" Madeline asks.

"Like a baby, thank you."

Madeline raises a cup. "Coffee?"

"Yes, please." I accept it and blow on the surface before taking a sip.

Sean kisses Madeline on the cheek. "Morning, Mom," he says, stealing a croissant out of her hand and adjusting the camera around his neck before ushering me to the front door.

"Sean, she hasn't had breakfast yet," Madeline exclaims.

I place the coffee mug on the table. "It's fine. I don't normally eat breakfast anyway."

Derek perks up. "I thought you doctors proclaim that breakfast is the most important meal of the day?"

"Not this doctor!" I flash a bright smile at Victoria and Katie.

"Where are you going, Sean? I made plans for us girls later today."

Sean pops his head back into the room. "I'll have her back before midday, but this morning she's all mine."

"You're not taking more photos of raccoons again, are you, son?" Clifford asks.

Sean sighs. "No, Dad."

"Thanks for the coffee! Have a great morning, everyone!" I say, following Sean out of the room.

My white trainers crush against the rocky trail with every step I take. I stop and watch Sean take photos of the stunning views of cliffs, coves, and wildflowers.

"Why are we here again?" I ask.

Sean grins and lowers his camera. "The less time spent with the family, the better. Besides, isn't it amazing?"

"So, you're a rugged outdoorsman at heart."

Sean laughs. "What type of guy did you think I was?"

I narrow my eyes and pause in thought before continuing. "The rich playboy type, I guess."

"Ha! How presumptuous of you. I'll have you know *I'm* not that rich. My parents are. And while it might be true I've dated a few women in my time, I'm not that guy anymore." He gives me a stern but teasing look. "You know, I'm over being typecast as the playboy."

"Okay, okay, I believe you. I'm sorry I ever thought that about you."

Sean affords me a forgiving smile. Then he briskly guides me to the edge of the trail so a mountain biker can pass.

"Thank you," I say, enjoying his warm hand wrapped around my arm. He smiles and lets me go. "You seem like you're in your element with that camera. Maybe you should take it more seriously."

"Thanks, but I missed my shot at making a career of this a long time ago. I turned down a gallery show just to prove to my dad that I was committed to the company. Besides, the company pays me more."

"Seems like a waste of talent to me."

He laughs. "Alright, what about you? I can tell you're a fantastic actress."

I smile, brushing away a pesky bug. "Thanks. I wish my agent thought that."

"Why did you give up acting?"

I groan. "Long story. Let's just say you're not the only one who makes stupid mistakes that come back to haunt you. Who knew I'd be turning thirty, working as a checkout girl by day and the fake fiancée of a meat mogul by night?"

I jerk my chin towards a nearby bench. "Mind if we take a break? It's hot."

He happily sits next to me and gulps some water while I admire the nature surrounding us. I sigh.

"A casting agent told me years ago that if I could be happy doing anything rather than acting, then choose that. And now I wish I listened. Show biz is not for the faint-hearted. But my heart was set on it. It's not like I wanted to be famous or rich even. I wanted to tell stories and portray lives that could inspire people. It made me happy and gave me purpose."

My demeanor wilts. "And now I'll never have a chance to show everyone my true potential. My purpose now is to make sure my dog doesn't starve to death. I might not be a CEO, a famous actress, or an influencer, but at least I earn an honest living and get to come home to a dog that loves me. And you know what? I'm starting to be okay with that."

I feel his intense gaze wash all over me. I turn to him. "What? Am I being weird again?"

"Not at all," he says with a deep gentle tone. "I think we're all actors in our own way. Everyone is pretending to be some-body they're not, even if they don't realize it. Pretending to be happy, pretending to have it all together, pretending to be … in love."

The sounds of cheery hikers and the lush green nature blur. All I can focus on is his sharp, interested gaze. My sparkly eyes travel to his mouth. I bite my lower lip and swallow. He leans closer to me, then wrenches his head away and continues, "I mean, look at my parents. If you haven't noticed already, they despise each other."

"They seem happy to me. My parents bicker all the time, but deep down I know they love each other."

"Right, but mine are like this in front of company. You should see them when no one is around. That's why they haven't slept in the same bed since I was seventeen. But do you think they will go their separate ways and find true happiness? No. They're too wrapped up in what people think of them. They must be seen to have it all together so they can socialize with people who 'matter', whatever that even means."

Blindsided by his passionate insight, I think of him in a new way. A way that makes me feel like I will ruin my chances of getting the money if I don't control my desires.

Sean looks at me contentedly. He smiles and raises his cam-era in my direction. "Stay there," he orders.

I play with my hair and try not to pull a duck face.

"Just act natural."

I loosen up while he snaps away and continues talking. "I guess that's why I like working on the farms with the animals. They're real and transparent. There are no games. They don't know how to manipulate. They're ..." he lowers the camera and looks into my eyes, "... beautiful."

I can't help but blush, fluttering my lashes. A long silence grows as we lock eyes like magnets to metal. Then he yells, *"Spider!"*

I leap from the bench and scream, flicking my hands around my body hysterically.

"Relax, it's gone!" Sean exclaims.

I hold perfectly still, paranoid that the spider is on me. "Are you sure?"

"I'm sure," he says, with growing dimples.

I breathe a sigh of relief and sit back down while Sean laughs. I playfully push his chest before folding my arms. "Jerk! There was no spider, was there?"

"There was, I swear!" His easy laugh fades into a warm smile. "I enjoyed your little dance."

I whack him across his arm and smile. "You know what, apart from the spider, I'm glad you brought me here. I forgot what it's like being around nature." I remember something I've been curious about. "Ah, don't take this the wrong way, but if you love animals so much why do you condemn them to their final death just so mere humans can eat them?"

A hefty chuckle escapes him, which I find utterly sexy. "I see your point. But that's the law of nature. At least we give them a good life."

"Then why do you want the CEO position, if you're happy where you are?"

"What? And let Derek have all the glory? I've watched Derek be the golden boy my whole life while I existed in his shadow. He's always been smarter than me, better at sports than me—"

"He's not better *looking* than you."

An amused smile plays on his lips as he rolls his shoulders. "Thanks, I'll take that. But I don't think my looks played a part in getting this far." He fixes his eyes on mine. "You did though." He leans closer and takes my sweaty hand. "I can be someone my parents are proud of because of you, Sal."

His piercing gaze dances between my hopeful eyes and parting lips. Without filtering my thoughts, my voice shoots out before I can stop it. "Even though I'm just doing it for the money?"

Instantly, he lets go of my hand and turns his attention away. I can't believe what a fool I am for bringing up the money! His demeanor takes a sullen dive, and I feel him disconnect. The hot air grows cold. I don't know what to say.

"I'm sorry, that came out wrong!"

"Don't worry. You'll get your money." Sean stands up and walks back down the trail.

Left on the bench alone, I'm confused and angry at having ruined such a magical moment. I pick up my pace to follow him and we walk back to the car in silence.

"Sean!" I yell across the front lawn, where he strides yards ahead of me. He stops just short of the deck.

"Did I offend you back there? I feel like you're ignoring me."

"Nope. This is a business deal, nothing more. Why would I be upset about that?" His tone is cold and icy, like his eyes.

I scrunch up my face. "I don't know. You tell me?"

"Nothing to tell."

"Then why do I feel like you're giving me the cold shoulder? *You're* the one using me, remember? If you weren't trying so hard to please your dad and outshine Derek, we wouldn't be in this mess."

"Mess? Ha! Well, feel free to leave this *mess* anytime! You're the one who called me, *remember?* You're the one getting twenty thousand dollars!" The harsh tone in his voice makes me step back.

His eyes flick to Derek and Victoria, who are lingering on the deck. I can see Derek tilt his head to Victoria with a gleeful smirk.

Sean lowers his voice and puts on a fake smile. "Now laugh and hug me like you mean it."

Animatedly, I leap into his arms and laugh as if he has just told me a joke. Our cozy facade is interrupted by Madeline's voice resonating from the doorway. "Sally dear, you ready?"

I flash Sean an apologetic smile before I join Madeline and Victoria, already dressed in designer clothing, and I mentally prepare myself for what they have planned for me.

I sit in a massage chair in a tranquil beauty spa trying to enjoy my pedicure. But all I can hear are Madeline and Victoria next to me babbling about the latest fashion trends on the runway.

"You're awfully quiet, Sally," Madeline says.

"It's not every day I get fussed over like this," I reply.

"Oh really? We do this every month, don't we, Victoria?"

"At least." Victoria glances over at me, "No signs of cold feet, Sally?"

"Um, no, my feet are pretty warm thanks, Victoria."

Victoria throws Madeline a smirk, and they both laugh. "That's not what I meant. It's not long till you say 'I do.' It's perfectly normal to have doubts."

"Oh. Nope. No doubts here. My feet are very much on fire!"

"I certainly had doubts about marrying Derek. But look at us now."

Madeline reaches for Victoria's hand. "I don't know a happier couple, myself."

"Nor do I Madeline. In saying that, marriage isn't for the weak. Sometimes I wonder why people do it at all! Most marriages end in heartbreak these days because there's so much temptation out there. We live in a throwaway society where everyone wants the easy way. Marriage is not easy!"

"Don't put her off, Victoria. I'm sure they'll be just fine. Won't you, Sally?"

I offer Madeline a weak smile and nod hesitantly. The spa lady approaches me with my favorite shade of baby-pink nail polish in her hands. "This one, ma'am?"

"Yes, please. It's so pretty!" I reply.

Madeline's eyes widen. "Sally! You can't have pink polish on your wedding day!" Madeline shoos the lady away with her hands. "Excuse me, change it to a French tip! Right now!"

"Certainly, ma'am," the spa lady nods in agreement and catches my sorrow-filled eyes as she leaves.

"Jolene's Bar?" I enquire curiously.

"You didn't think we'd let you get married without a bachelorette party, did you?" Madeline says, whipping a cheap bridal veil from her Louis Vuitton handbag and placing it on my head.

"Surprise!" Victoria opens the door to a bar adorned with red, white, and blue Fourth of July decorations. Rowdy patrons drink beer and eat peanuts and chicken wings. Drunk people bump crossing paths, and flailing bodies dance to the loud karaoke tunes that play from the back of the room.

I glance at Madeline. I didn't think she would agree to set her Jimmy Choos in a place like this. "Really?" I ask.

"Oh, I know, isn't it ghastly?! I couldn't get a reservation at Saffron Lodge at short notice, so Victoria insisted we come here." Madeline looks at Victoria. "This place is for louts, darling. I don't want to be seen here."

"Keep an open mind, Madeline." Victoria ushers us into the bar. "Come on. Drinks are on me tonight!"

Madeline purses her lips and raises a judgy eyebrow while she watches Billy, the chiseled bartender whose hair is pulled back in a short ponytail, serve us tequila shots. Then Victoria orders a bottle of champagne and some snacks before we sit around a reserved table near the stage. Billy brings the champagne over and pours for us. Before he leaves, he gives me a seductive wink. I glance down at the table and see a phone number scrawled on a napkin.

Victoria leans into me. "Think he's got the hots for you!"

I laugh it off and continue swaying my shoulders to the sounds of a woman butchering Celine Dion's *That's The Way It Is*. Victoria leans in again. "You know, I wouldn't blame you if you wanted one last hurrah." I stop moving and try to conceal my shock from Madeline, who is in her own little world, clapping her hands out of sync to the beat.

"Victoria, I take my marriage to Sean seriously."

Victoria shrugs and raises her glass. "Well, bottoms up then!" We clink our glasses, and when I see Victoria narrow her deceptive eyes, I know I must be careful about what I say.

I'm surprised to see Madeline having so much fun in this boisterous environment that seems far below her usual standards. But then again, two tequila shots and a bottle of champagne will loosen anyone up. Madeline pulls us onto the dance floor, and we shimmy and twerk until an energetic host mounts the stage.

"Ladies and gentlemen, are we all enjoying ourselves?"

The crowd roars with so much enthusiasm that the host has to calm us down. "We'll resume our karaoke, but for now, I would like to invite a special someone who is getting married in two days to come to the stage."

I gulp and shoot daggers at Victoria, who's smirking. *Oh fuck.*

"Please welcome ... Sally *soon-to-be* Maxwell!"

I freeze on the dance floor and gasp while everyone around cheers me on, including Madeline and Victoria.

"Oh, no. Nope, not doing it!" I say stubbornly.

Victoria pushes me to the front. "Oh, yes, you are."

The crowd chants my name. *Sal-ly, Sal-ly.* I don't want to disappoint them (or Madeline, who's attempting a wolf whistle) so I walk onto the stage and allow the host to guide me to a black chair placed front and center. The lights switch off, leaving everyone in the dark. Then a spotlight beams down on me, and *Bad Case of Loving You* by Robert Palmer starts to play. Moments later, Billy bursts out from behind the red velvet curtain, dressed in a doctor's coat with a stethoscope slung around his neck.

The crowd goes crazy! And I can see why when I get an eyeful of his oily bronze manscaped chest. He circles me and performs an elaborate dance routine that showcases his unusual flexibility, and which involves checking my heart with the stethoscope. He rips his coat off like an angry gorilla and reveals his buff physique. His naked buns of steel entertain the audience, while the large bulge of his G-string (featuring an embroidered syringe) makes me squirm.

He wraps his legs over mine and whispers in my ear, "Do you want to be vaccinated tonight?"

I see Madeline shriek, next to her Victoria laughs. Billy thrusts his pelvis, and my head pulls back like a turtle retreating into its shell. He puts his hands behind his head and flexes, then grabs my hands and places them on his chest. I leap off the chair like a scared little deer wanting this to be over.

"Playing hard to get, I see?" Billy teases.

"Eww!" I keep my distance. The cat-and-mouse game delights the crowd and the laughter and cheers reach a fever pitch.

Billy bucks his pelvis to the music, moving toward me where I stand near the edge of the stage. With every thrust he makes, I take a step back, until a final thrust propels me off the stage and into the air.

"Oww!" I scream, as my body hits the floor.

The music stops, and I hear gasps of horror and whispers. Billy's eyes peep down at me. Fueled by embarrassment and tequila, I spring to my feet and address the crowd, "I'm okay!"

Chapter 18

Sean

I'M SPRAWLED OUT ON a leather Winchester couch in the living room. I watch the clock above the mantel tick while Derek shuffles through paperwork on a table behind me.

"What's the matter, Sean? Missing your fiancée already?" Derek asks.

"No. They're just later than I thought they'd be."

"Relax. I told Vic to look after her. I'm sure the locals will look after her too."

I sit up and face Derek. "What's that supposed to mean?"

"She's a beautiful girl. I'm sure she gets lots of attention."

My mouth gapes open. Suddenly the thought of Sal meeting other men makes my skin crawl.

Derek laughs. "Relax! Sheesh, you're the one she's marrying. You've got nothing to worry about."

"I'm not worried," I mutter, looking at the clock again.

"If you're serious about joining me as CEO, why don't you be useful and help me figure out how we can raise our revenue?"

I join him, and we flip through documents together until our attention is interrupted by raucous singing that gets louder as the girls barge through the back door in a wobbly state.

"Why hello, my handsome sons. I hope you didn't wait up for us?" Mom yells.

Derek and I share a suspicious glance before I approach Mom, who's draped on Sal's shoulder. "Mom, are you drunk?"

She slides off Sal's shoulder. "Not drunk! *Been* drinking."

Sal and Victoria laugh and help her to her feet. I take Sal's hand. "It's late. I'm taking you to bed."

"Relax, what are you, my dad?" Sal says, brushing my hand away.

Derek laughs right before a loud burp escapes Sal's throat. Everyone stares at her and she covers her mouth with her hand.

She looks at me guiltily, "Okay, let's go."

I pick her up and throw her over my shoulder.

"I can walk, Sean. I'm drunk, not dead!"

I grin at everyone before whisking her up the stairs. "Good night, all."

Derek

Mom excuses herself, still singing as she climbs the stairs, and Victoria joins me at the table.

"So, you did get her drunk?" I quietly ask.

Victoria grins, and sways in her chair.

"Did you get anything out of her?"

"No, Derek. I even hired Billy to seduce her as you asked, but she didn't take the bait. She's in love with your brother.

Everyone loved her." She lowers her tone and slurs her words. "Her and her perky boobs."

"Don't tell me you like her?"

"No, Derek. But I can see why Sean does."

"What are we going to do now?!"

Victoria rolls her tipsy eyes. "I dunno, go to bed."

I slam my pen down on the table with a growl.

Sal

"No peeking!" I chirp, scoping the room from behind the ensuite door.

Sean half-smiles and closes his eyes. After he pulls the blanket up to his chin, I tiptoe past him like a naughty fairy trying not to faceplant on the floor.

I snuggle into bed and turn off the bedside lamp. "You can look now!"

"Pink's your color, you know," he says.

I throw a pillow in his direction. "You looked, you are bad!"

"I'm sorry, I couldn't help it! When someone tells me to do something, I automatically want to do the opposite."

I laugh and reminisce about my night. "I haven't had a night like that since—" I stop abruptly as I realize I haven't heard from Fran or Piper. My bubbly mood fizzles away into the bed.

"You okay over there?" Sean asks.

"Yeah, I'm okay. I just miss my friends, I guess."

"Mom told me you weren't inviting any of them *or* your parents to the wedding?"

"I didn't see the point in lying to two sets of families, if you get my drift."

Sean's voice softens. "Yeah, fair call."

"Besides, my best friends think I'm crazy for marrying some-one I've just met. And well, I think my parents would probably just be happy I'm not a lesbian."

He lets out one of his sexy belly laughs. "You told your friends about us?"

The way he uses the word *us* gives me more comfort than the delicious Egyptian cotton sheets I'm snuggled between. "It just came out. Not the fake part. They know I'm getting married on Monday and I still haven't heard from them. Some friends, huh?"

"Ironically, I think good friends *wouldn't* be happy you were marrying a stranger."

"Well, when you put it like that," my light-hearted laugh fades into a long pause. "Hey, um. Sorry about earlier today."

"No, I'm the one who should be sorry. I shouldn't have raised my voice at you. You were right, you know. We wouldn't be here if I weren't so wrapped up in proving myself to my dad. But you know what? I'm glad we are, otherwise I wouldn't have met you."

Warm tingles spread through my body, and silence fills the room as I close my eyes.

"Sal?"

My parched eyes struggle open. My mouth moves like a horse's chewing its bit. Disoriented, I get out of bed and slowly walk along the dark hallway and down the stairs, where I bumble around till I find a light switch. I fetch a glass of water from the kitchen, which I gulp down in one go. As I walk past the living room, I can just make out the clock, which reads three am. I climb the dark staircase, squinting to see where I'm going, and quietly slip back into bed. Not long after I close my eyes, I feel a warm sensation. A sudden movement jars my eyes wide open.

"Sean?" I hesitantly whisper. "Is that you?" A pair of arms swallow me from behind. I hear a snort followed by a small groan that does *not* sound like Sean.

"Madeline, it isn't like you to come to me at this hour."

I try to control my panting breaths, but they only quicken when Clifford tightens his embrace, leaving me with no way out.

"Are you wearing silk?" he asks.

A slight squeal escapes me as I pin my eyes shut.

"Have you lost weight?" Clifford asks, stroking my nightgown.

Oh no oh no oh no. I bite down on my lip.

"Maddie?"

"Yes?" I squeak fearfully, dreading what's to come.

He quickly releases me and the lamp switches on, illuminating my scared squirrel-about-to-be-roadkill expression. "*Sally?!* What on earth!"

I raise my hands in a shushing gesture, so he doesn't alert anyone to *the most* embarrassing moment of my life. "I'm sorry, I'm so sorry. I must have been sleepwalking and got the wrong room, I swear!"

Clifford raises a palm in the air. "This is a little strange, Sally."

"I know. I don't know how I got here. I'm so sorry."

Clifford tears his eyes away from me and looks down. After a long awkward silence, he mutters, "You need to leave."

Sean

I wake up to Sal's demented roosters and laugh at the sight of her spread out with her mouth wide open, snoring. "Sal?" I raise my voice. "Sally!"

I throw my pillow at her, and with a little snort, she wakes up. "Where am I?"

"You're with me."

"Oh."

"Can you please get a different alarm tone? My ears feel taken advantage of!"

"Oh, sorry!" She reaches across to the bedside table and turns it off. Then I see her glance in the phone's reflection before she leaps up and dashes to the ensuite.

"You alright, Sal?"

"Yup!" she calls, closing the door.

Sal

I run the faucet and splash water over my dehydrated face, pinch my cheeks, apply a little mascara, and flatten my wild hair with my hands. *There is no way he can see me like this!* I compose myself and then open the door to find Sean in my bed!

"Ah, what are you doing, Sean?"

"Quick, get in!"

Wow, maybe my *au naturel* look really does it for him.

"Wakey wakey, love birds. Are we all decent in there?" *Shit!* As soon as I hear Madeline's voice through the door, I dive into bed, where I'm scooped up into Sean's arms.

He looks down at me. "Did you just put makeup on?"

"*No!*—Come in, Madeline!"

Madeline enters the room with a tray of freshly brewed coffee. "Good morning!"

"Morning, Mom."

"Morning, Madeline."

"Aw, aren't you two just the sweetest—the last day my son will be a bachelor! I never thought I would see this day." She places the tray on the bed and sits next to me. "Drink up, Sally, because if you're feeling anything like I am, you'll need coffee."

"Thanks, Madeline, you read my mind. Last night was fun, but I'm paying for it now."

"Not as much fun as tomorrow will be. Now, up and at 'em because we have a big day ahead. Preparations are already underway." Madeline's eyes fall upon the comforter on the couch. "Did someone sleep on the sofa last night?"

Sean quickly answers. "No, we just got too hot. We threw a blanket off the bed."

"Oh! Very well then."

Clifford pops his head through the door. I gasp as I remember sleepwalking into his room. I draw the sheets up to my chin and offer him a small smile that I hope he translates into *please don't say anything!*

"Morning, Dad," Sean says.

"Don't mind me. I just came in to make sure Sally got home safely." Clifford winks at me, "And here she is, safe and sound."

Madeline cuts in. "Right, Clifford, chop-chop, we have lots of work to do today. Let's give them their privacy."

As soon as they leave, I look at Sean. "Sean, have you thought about what this will do to your family business if anyone finds out?"

"They won't find out. No one suspects a thing. Even Derek's left us alone."

"I feel sick," I say, still comfortably in his arms like we've been a couple for years.

"Me too," he replies, rubbing my shoulders. "Me too."

I look up and study his face. His magnetizing eyes draw my lips toward his. I feel him squeeze me into his chest, and I can tell he's about to kiss me. Before he has the chance, I haul my head over the side of the bed and barf all over the floor.

"Oh my god! Did you just throw up?" he asks with repulsion in his voice. I hear him dry reach and open a window. I manage to mutter a few words.

"I'm so sorry."

He sits next to me, holding my hair while he rubs my back. I tilt my head to the side and catch his smile. "Told you I felt sick."

Sean

I scrub away at the floor, scrunching up my face from the stench. Sal opens the ensuite door, and I look up to see her with a towel around her wet lithe body. I gulp and scrub the floor harder. "Feeling better?" I ask, trying not to look at her.

"I think I need to take a walk."

I admire her briefly. "Good idea. I think I'll take a cold shower."

Chapter 19

Sal

Striding out to the front lawn, I'm mesmerized by the enchanting transformation. A big, beautiful marquee decorated with red and blue ribbon takes center stage on the lawn. Rows of white chairs are on each side of a long red carpet that my very own feet will walk down in twenty-four hours. Caterers set up their stations, and Madeline and Victoria are ordering florists around.

"Who ordered these flowers? I asked for lilies, not cherry blossoms!" Madeline exclaims. I avoid eye contact with her and change my direction. I can't endure talking to anyone, and my head pounds from the chaos around me. Next minute I'm face to face with Clifford.

"Sally." His tone is low and he avoids eye contact.

"Clifford! Sorry about last night. I tend to sleepwalk when I've had a few too many."

He conjures up a smile and meets my gaze. "It'll be our little secret. But please—don't ever do that again."

Not a snowman's chance in hell! "Thank you, I won't," I promise fervently.

The noise around me caves in, along with the reality that everyone I can see is setting up a *wedding* for *me*. How did I go from Single Sal to getting married?! I excuse myself and pick up my pace across the lawn toward the dock.

"Sally darling! Where are you going?"

"I just need some fresh air, Madeline. I'll be right back!"

I briskly walk to the end of the dock and sit down with my legs dangling over the side. My eyes close as I take a deep breath and open again as I exhale. I haven't had a moment to myself all weekend, and I enjoy the stillness of the tranquil lake and the sounds of the whistling birds. My peace is interrupted by my phone beeping. I whip it out of my pocket, and a group chat from Fran and Piper flashes across my screen:

We love you, Sal! Is everything okay? xxx

Reading those words fills my heart with joy, and I wish I could tell them the truth. But I don't know what the truth is anymore. I watch the waterbirds and regretfully decide not to message back. Instead, I make a call.

"Carlos?"

"Chica! What took you so long?"

"First of all, how's Oscar?"

"He's still alive. We've had a blast together. And you're not the only one going through a little transformation."

My eyes narrow. "Care to elaborate?" Visions fly through my mind of Oscar with pink fur, *rhinestoned to the gods, darling.*

"Nope! I want the tea. Give it to me. What's been happening?"

"I don't know if I can go through with this, Carlos."

"What happened? Is it all going to plan?"

"Yes, no one suspects a thing. It's been better than I'd hoped."

"What, actually, is the problem then?"

I am silent, thinking. I don't know what *actually* the problem is.

"You've fallen for him, haven't you?"

"What! No."

"Uh-*huh*."

"Okay, maybe a little. I didn't think faking love would be this easy. I don't know what's real and what isn't anymore!"

"Sal, you have one more day, after that you can sort out whatever feelings you have for this guy. Stay focused baby."

"I don't even know what my goal is anymore. At first, it was to find love before my birthday. Then it was to get the money. And now, neither of those matter. This family has *accepted* me. If they find out I'm a fraud, I'll ruin everything."

"Simple! Don't let them find out. Just keep doing what you've been doing until you say 'I do'. Got it?"

"Got it."

"I fly out first thing in the morning. So, hold tight."

"Thanks, Carlos."

Feeling mentally refreshed and ready to take on whatever comes my way, I confidently walk back to the lawn and slow my pace when I see Sean twirling Katie around. Seeing him like that makes my stomach flutter, and I can tell he would make a great dad. *Dad?* Why am I thinking about having children with him? *This fresh lake air is making me lose the plot.*

"He's a fantastic uncle, isn't he?"

My head spins around to see Madeline holding two wedding bouquets.

"Madeline! You frightened me."

"Now, what do you think? Cherry blossoms or tiger lilies?"

"I love the cherry blossoms."

"Oh?" Madeline says disappointedly. Her eyes skim to Sean, running toward us. "Let's ask Sean."

"Sean, what do you think? Sal likes the cherry blossoms, but the tiger lilies are much superior, don't you think?"

Sean washes his easy eyes over me. "Ah, I think Sal's right. I like the cherry blossoms, Mom."

"Oh, I see. Very well then."

I notice a row of chairs being added to the seating layout. "Madeline. How many people are we expecting tomorrow? I thought it would be a small wedding—just the family?"

"Oh, darling. My youngest son only gets married once. I've invited a few guests. Don't worry. I've got it all sorted." Madeline's eyes focus on the staff and she rushes off. "Excuse me! Those don't go there!"

"Your mom is really in her element, isn't she?"

He laughs. "Controlling people is what she does best."

We walk side by side to the nearest table and are momentarily entertained watching Madeline frantically order people around.

"Looks like I'm getting married in front of a bunch of strangers tomorrow."

"If it makes you feel any better, they're strangers to me too. Half of them are probably business associates my parents want to impress."

I place a hand on his arm. "I'm so sorry about this morning. I'm so embarrassed!"

He laughs. "I must say, I've seen ... shall we say, some intriguing sides of you since we've met."

"Thanks for going easy on me. But what you want to say is, you've seen some gross and unladylike sides."

He laughs again. "Well—"

I cut in to save his breath. "I swear you've seen me at my worst."

"I look forward to seeing you at your best then. It can only get better from here, right?"

I grin. "You would think."

Sean crosses his arms and stretches out his legs. "And for the record, you didn't look that bad this morning."

"I don't know what you're talking about."

"I know you went to the bathroom to put on makeup." He looks away from me and laughs. "Trust me. You look good in the morning compared to some women I've dated. One minute I'm going to bed with Kim Kardashian, and the next I'm waking up with Ronald McDonald."

I blush, looking down at my feet, holding in an urge to laugh.

He fastens his eyes on mine. "You don't need anyone to tell you you're beautiful."

Light bolts burst through my heart, my cheeks feel like they're on fire, and I want to erupt with joy. No man has ever told me I look beautiful without makeup. Makeup is my secret weapon in life. While some people reach for liquor for a confidence boost, I reach for liquid eyeliner. Every time I feel insecure, all I have to do is add another gossamer-thin layer of makeup, and my insecurities evaporate. Although I also use makeup creatively to enhance my features, I mainly use it to hide who I am. I don't truly believe I have anything to offer a man without my good looks. But for the first time in my life, I feel comfortable in my skin.

I smile warmly and enjoy the natural comfort he gives me, even in such a fabricated scenario. "Did you ever hear back from your ex?" I ask.

"Ha! If an *I never want to see you again* message on Facebook counts, right before she blocked me. Then yep, sure did!"

He thinks. His expression grows smug. "Why, would it be a problem if we were still in touch?"

"No. *Why would it* be a problem?"

He chuckles and shakes his head slightly. "I don't know, you tell me, Sal?"

I screw up my mouth and contemplate admitting how I feel, but I can't face another embarrassment if he rejects me. "Nothing to tell."

The twinkle in his eye diminishes, and his tone lowers. "That's right. You're just here for the money."

I pin my eyes on his. "Sean, we've talked about this. You're oversimplifying."

He grabs my hand. "Don't worry. I'm just being a jerk. So, what about you? I never did officially ask if you were seeing anyone?"

"For a guy who's seen me at my worst, do you have to ask?"

"Come on, Sal. I know I've seen some unflattering things, but I also know you're not always like that. And even if you were, it's rather entertaining."

"I guess I've always dated the wrong guys."

"Is there such thing as the right one, though?"

"I like to think there is."

Our intimate bubble is interrupted by a life vest crashing against Sean's legs. "You're up, champ!" Derek calls.

Sean lets go of my hand and raises his palms in the air. "Oh no, no, no."

"What? You afraid you'll lose again?" Derek's eyes size me up.

"How 'bout you, Sally? You in?"

"Me? What are we doing?"

Derek points toward the center of the lake. "See that buoy out there?" I nod. "Every summer, we race to that buoy and back. I kick his scrawny butt every time, don't I, Sean?"

Sean shakes his head. "This summer is a bit different, Derek."

Victoria approaches in her black swimsuit, life vest in hand. "It's fun, Sally. You should join us!"

"Oh, I'm not a water person. I can't swim that well."

"There's no swimming involved. Just Sean and a jet ski," Victoria replies.

Derek eyeballs Sean. "What do you say, she might finally bring you some luck out there?"

I know this rivalry between them is unhealthy, but right now I want nothing more than for Sean to trounce Derek. "I'm in."

Derek claps his hands together and grins. "That's settled then. Loser mans the grill tonight."

Sean picks the vest off the ground and stands up. "You'd better get your apron ready."

Sean

I sit on the bed, and with a few flicks of my fingers, I unbutton half my shirt and set my eyes on Sal. "You don't have to ride with me if you don't want to," I say. I can feel her eyes dance around my chest, and it amuses me.

"Nope. We are going to win this race together. Besides, I want to see the look on your brother's face when we kick his butt."

I stand up, take my shirt off and grin from ear to ear. "I knew there was a reason I'm marrying you."

Sal licks her lips and swallows before she speaks. "I'll get changed in the bathroom. Meet you at the dock?"

With a nod, I watch her close the ensuite door. I gaze out the window in profound thought. I didn't expect to feel the way I do about her. She's different from all the other women I've dated. When I'm with Sal, I feel like I have nothing to prove and everything to gain. My plan is taking a turn. The thing is, I'm not sure if it's a turn for better or for worse.

Chapter 20

Sal

"THERE SHE IS!" MADELINE exclaims, prompting Sean to look at me as I walk down the dock toward him in a yellow bikini I secretly hope he likes. His eyes are glued to me, and I can tell by his sultry grin that he's admiring the view.

"It's a hot day, isn't it, everyone? I think it's supposed to get up to eighty-five today," Sean burbles.

Derek leers at me as I approach. "Right! Let's do this!" I say enthusiastically.

Derek and Victoria put on their life vests, and Sean helps with mine. I can do it myself, but I let him take the lead. He zips the front up, and my hands start to shake. I'm unsure if it's because Sean's proximity makes me nervous or because I'm afraid of deep water.

He slides three fingers between my body and the vest. "Perfect fit. Now, I must warn you. I go fast."

"That's the whole point, right?"

Derek and Victoria wait on their jet ski and watch as I settle myself behind Sean. I tuck my legs behind his and wrap my arms around his waist. He pulls my hands in tighter. "You're going to need a better grip than that," he says dominantly.

He lines up our jet ski with Derek's, then nods to Clifford.

"Derek. Are you ready?" Clifford yells from the dock.

"Ready, Dad!"

Derek shoots a sideways glance at Sean. "How about you, Sean? Ready to lose?"

Sean glares back with a determination that makes me wonder what I'm in for. I gaze toward the horizon where the buoy bobs up and down, then see Sean tighten his grip around the handlebars. "You ready, Sal?"

I squeak my assent and rest my cheek on his back, ready for take-off.

"Don't forget, boys, you must touch the buoy before returning, or you'll be disqualified!"

Madeline wishes me luck while Katie giggles in excitement. "Good luck, Mommy and Daddy!"

Clifford raises one arm in the air. "In three, two, one ..." he waves his hand down, "GO!"

Before I can suck in a breath, we're zooming through the water at lightning speed which causes my grip on Sean to loosen. The cold air rushes harshly across my face, and I shudder at the thought of developing a wind rash. From the corner of my watering eye, I see Derek and Victoria gunning behind us.

"Faster, Derek!" Victoria yells.

"Everything okay back there?" Sean calls.

"Yup!" I squeal, excited we're winning, but I'm struggling to hold on. The buoy is close, and now we're side by side with Derek and Victoria. The race is on. Derek surpasses us by a thread—Sean revs his engine in response, and I catapult into the air.

Sean

"Woohoo!" I exclaim, sheer excitement in my voice as I reach out to touch the buoy. "We did it, Sal!" I look over my shoulder, and Sal is gone. *"Sal!"*

Derek surges his jet ski up to mine and touches the buoy. Victoria throws me Sal's yellow bikini bottoms. "I think you forgot someone," she calls, barely containing her glee.

"Later, loser!" Derek crows, as he whizzes off toward the shore and victory.

"Sal!" I yell, frantically looking around. Then I see the top of her hand waving in the distance. With no time to lose, I head straight for her. I can hardly make out her face as it's smothered with wet hair, but I can sense her rage.

"Sal! I'm so sorry!"

She deliriously doggy paddles closer to the jet ski. When she gasps, I know she's seen her bikini bottoms in my hands. "Give me those!" she yells.

"Shit, sorry, I'm so sorry!" I throw them at her and awkwardly watch her try to put them back on. I want to get in the water and help but her expression is thunderous, so I decide to show emotional support instead. "You're doing great, Sal."

"Don't look!" she snarls, still struggling. After I get the all-clear, I haul her to refuge on the jet ski. I wipe the wet hair off her face, and she blinks to clear her vision. She doesn't have to speak for me to know that she's traumatized. She's shivering and her helpless demeanor makes me want to protect her. I wrap my arms around her and she looks up at me with such vulnerability it sets my heart on fire.

"I'm sorry we didn't win the race."

"I'm not." I place her in front of me and gently cradle her as I pilot the jet ski back to land.

Sal

Everyone cheers as we pull up to the dock.

Derek cackles. "Too bad little bro! Maybe next time."

The cheerful atmosphere rapidly changes as Sean leaps off the jet ski and storms toward him. "You didn't think to help her when you saw her in the water?"

"She had a life vest on. She was fine. If she weren't so light, she wouldn't have flown like that!" He turns to Victoria and scoffs, "No wonder her bikini bottoms fell off."

Sean reaches toward Derek, but his raging eyes cross to me. I wipe a tear from the corner of my eye and shake my head. "Forget about it, Sean."

"See. Don't be such a Serious Suzy." Derek puts his arm around Victoria's neck, and they head up the front lawn laughing victoriously. Clifford throws Sean a beach towel before joining Madeline and Katie.

"Better luck next time, Sally. And son—there's always next summer."

Sean sighs and helps me take my life vest off. I cross my arms over my chest and shiver. He wraps a towel around me and hugs me while rubbing his hands up and down my arms. "I'm so sorry, Sal."

He rests his chin on my head. Suddenly, I'm not so cold. A slow fiery burn in the pit of my stomach ignites a fire in my heart.

A loud whistle from the top of the lawn catches our attention. A dark haired man walks toward us with a confident swagger, wearing Ray Bans and a colorful summer shirt.

"Who's that?" I ask.

Sean squints. His concerned expression becomes a boisterous smile as the man gets closer. "*That* would be my best man," he declares.

Worry pulses through me as the man's charming smile seems way too familiar.

"Brady, you made it!" Sean exclaims across the lawn.

I look at Brady inquisitively, searching for a flash of recognition. I gasp as I realize where we met, and bury my head in Sean's chest, "Oh my god, I know him!"

"What? You know Brady?"

As he approaches, I scrunch up my face.

"I hope you're not talking about how ridiculously handsome I am—bring it in, brother!" Brady says, giving Sean a big man hug and a few playful punches. Then his gaze turns to me.

"And who's the bride-to-be?" He gives Sean a questioning look.

"Brady, I'd like you to meet Sally."

"Nice to meet you, Sally." Brady extends his hand to me. As we make eye contact, a vivid memory of him directing me on the set of the condom commercial floods back. I pray to the universe that he won't recognize me with shorter hair and less makeup.

"Pleasure to meet you, Brady." After a moment of silence, I step back, flick my eyes at Sean and give a fleeting smile to Brady. "I'm sorry, I've got to get changed. But I look forward to catching up with you later." I briskly head toward the house, but when I glance back I notice a disturbed look on Brady's face.

Sean

"What's that look for, Brady?" I ask.

"What *look?*" he replies.

I know he's holding back so I throw an arm around him and turn him away from the prying eyes of Derek, who's lurking on the deck.

"Come on, we have a lot to catch up on," I say, leading him down the dock.

"She's cute, bro. I'm happy for you," Brady says in a humorless tone.

I stop at the end of the dock and glare at him. "I sense a 'but' coming."

Brady shrugs his shoulders and lets his thoughts fly out of his mouth. "I just never thought you'd get married before me. Honestly, I never thought you'd get married at all! I thought you were dating that model. Now you're getting married to a doctor?"

I look serenely out over the lake. "Yup. It's a weird world."

Brady shakes his head and contorts his mouth. "Man, you know what, I'm sure I've seen her before. I just don't know where."

I close my eyes, inhale, and sit down with my back against a wooden pole. "Sit down, Brady."

"Sounds serious." He sits down opposite me.

"I'm going to tell you this, but you have to swear you won't tell a soul."

Brady lowers his shades to the tip of his nose, and the piercing sun accentuates his eager hazel eyes. "Sounds juicy. Give it to me!"

"I'm not getting married."

"And ... I'm not following."

"Well, I am but it's"—I lower my voice—"fake."

"*What the*—" Brady clamps a hand over his mouth.

"I met her at ... well, never mind, that's not important. She's an actress I hired to pretend to be my fiancée. We weren't planning on actually getting married. It just got out of hand."

"Oh, shit, bro! The condom commercial I directed! *That's her!*"

I squint my eyes in confusion. "Condom commercial?"

"Oh, man, what a flop that was. Nearly ruined my career."

I raise an eyebrow and decide not to ask any more questions.

"I knew this was too good to be true. I mean, you never wanted to get married."

"Shhh, can you lower your voice please?"

"What? You afraid the birds will hear?"

I cross my arms. "Who said I never wanted to get married?"

Brady laughs. "You did! You're the biggest player I know! You're still in your prime. Why would you want to give up all the attention you receive in favor of one person forever?"

"Ruthless bro! I am not a player, thank you."

Brady gives me an incredulous look.

"Okay, fine, maybe I was a little. I just hadn't found my person yet."

Brady puts his hand on my forehead. "Are you feeling alright? Do you need a *doctor?*"

I swipe his hand away, letting out a low chuckle. "It's true. I do want to settle down one day. I'll be turning thirty-four soon. I'm over the dating games."

"Looks like Sally's made an impression on you," Brady mumbles.

"No," I reply defensively.

"Ha! You *do* like her. I saw you cuddling up to her before. There are some things you cannot fake."

"This is a business deal."

"Uh-huh."

The corner of my mouth curls. "She is beautiful, though, isn't she?"

Brady laughs, shaking his head. "Sean. Why go through all this? What's in it for you?"

"Dad was going to sign the firm over to Derek tomorrow."

"Right, and you wanted your slice of the pie. But after our rowdy trip to Vegas with the boys, you were demoted. But somehow you think marrying a 'doctor' will prove your worth again?"

"Something like that."

Brady flings an arm in the air, clicking his fingers. "*Boom!* This is wilder than the movies I direct. If you pull this off, you'll be a goddamn legend."

"More like a really good liar. If my family find out the truth—"

Brady cuts me off. "I hear you. We'll be planning a funeral instead of a wedding. Don't worry. I've got your back."

Sal

· ❤ · ❤ · ❤ · ❤ · ❤ ·

I sit on the end of the bed, fresh out of the shower, with a towel wrapped around me. I strum my fingers anxiously on my thigh and leap up when the door opens.

Sean walks in with an easy laugh. "Relax, it's only me. Were you expecting the boogieman or something?"

"Something. Well?!"

Sean calmly takes both my hands and stares directly into my eyes. "You were right. He does remember you."

I let go of his hands and sit back on the bed. "I knew it! What the heck are we going to do, Sean?"

He joins me on the bed. "Don't worry. He won't say a thing."

"How can you be sure? How do you even know him?"

"Relax. He's been directing and producing our Maxwell's commercials for years. He's my best man for a reason. We can trust him." As he speaks his eyes sweep over my body. He runs a hand through his hair, then leaps up and takes a white shirt from the closet. "I'm going to start the grill. You come down when you're ready."

I reply with a nod. Just before he shuts the door, he pops his head back into the room. "Oh, and Sal."

"Yeah?"

"Eat the sausages with the green herbs in them."

Chapter 21

Sal

"DINNER SMELLS YUMMY!" I chirp, stepping out onto the deck in my pink ruffled Gucci dress. The cooking is in full swing. Sounds of sizzling meat hiss from the grill. Wine and whiskey are cheerfully consumed, and Katie twirls herself to the classical music that weaves between the animated conversations.

Sean turns around, his face glistening from the heat. He blinks to clear the steam from his eyes and drops his tongs. Brady laughs and picks them up, triumphantly making for the grill. Sean smiles at me before he reaches out snatches the tongs back.

I politely greet Clifford and Derek on my way to join the ladies who are standing at the edge of the lawn, dressed elegantly and drinking glasses of wine.

"I love your dress, Sally!" Madeline says as she pours me a glass.

"Where did you get it?" Victoria asks with a hint of jealousy.

I look across the deck at Sean, who's still staring at me. I smile at him before answering. "It's Gucci, actually."

"The girl's got taste," Victoria says, raising a laminated eyebrow.

Madeline smiles and turns her head to indicate the picturesque wedding venue. "What do you think, Sally?"

"It's stunning! Thank you, Madeline."

"I thought you'd love it," Madeline says proudly.

Sean and Brady put the large platters on the outdoor dining table and clink their drinks together before Sean clears his throat. "Dinner is now served."

Everyone happily takes their places, and the delicious aromas promise a scrumptious meal. Brady gives me a wink on the sly as I take my place between him and Sean. The rest of the family pass around various cuts of meat and Mediterranean salads.

Madeline puts her hands together. "All right. Bless this food. Amen, everybody! Dig in!" She glances at Sean and Brady. "Thank you, boys, this looks wonderful!"

Sean responds by raising his glass of water toward her, then shoots a fiery look at Derek, who's extending the steak across the table to me.

"No thank you, Derek," I say, eyeing up the sausages in front of me. "I think I might try these."

Derek's face screws up. "What are they anyway, Sean? They don't look like ours."

Sean points his fork at his brother before stabbing it into a sausage and placing it on his plate. "That's because they're a new recipe."

"Huh?"

Katie takes a bite. "Yum! These sausages are so yummy, Daddy."

"Give me one of those." Derek dubiously puts one on his plate and starts eating it.

Clifford extends his plate. "Over here, son."

Sean looks at me with a cheeky grin, then watches everyone devour his new creation.

"These are delicious, son," Clifford says.

Madeline chimes in. "They *are* scrummy, aren't they."

"When did you come up with the recipe?" Victoria asks.

Sean looks at me then back to Victoria. "It's one I've been working on for a while."

Derek chews with suspicion. "Hang on. Something's not right."

The whole table looks at Derek. "These aren't made out of meat, are they?"

I swallow my mouthful and gratefully squeeze Sean's leg. "They taste like meat, though. Good job, babe!"

Derek's face has horror all over it. "Why on earth would you make sausages that aren't meat?"

Sean flashes him a smile. "It's the new craze, Derek."

"That's absurd! What vegetarian would want to eat something that looks and tastes like meat? I've never understood it!" Derek exclaims.

"Like it or not, that is our competition. Especially in LA. If we're to keep our edge, then maybe this is a concept we should explore when we're partners."

"Ha! We're in the meat industry, brother. Our customers aren't grass-eating vegans. *Not* having it!"

Madeline clears her throat and smiles at Katie. "Are you excited you'll be a flower girl tomorrow, Katie-pie?"

"Yes, Grandma. I'm going to look so pretty!"

"You sure are, Katie," I say, smiling at her.

I catch Derek's burning eyes on me. "Sally, I tried to add you on Facebook, but I couldn't find you."

"That's because I'm not on it. Or any social media for that matter. I like to keep a private life. I'm too busy to worry about what other people are having for lunch."

His bold tone dissolves. "Yes, trying to save lives, I suppose."

Victoria perks up. "I wish we weren't on it. But we have to connect with our customers. Sadly, social media is at the forefront of our business, isn't it, darling?" Victoria looks at Derek for an answer but he hastily dismisses her before his cunning eyes blaze in my direction.

"You said you went to Albert Einstein College, right?" he asks.

I finish chewing and look across at him. "Yes."

"I talked to Tom Reilly, who said he doesn't remember you. I thought that was a bit strange, considering it would have only been a year ago that you were in his class."

Brady takes a swig of beer, and I see Sean's jaw clench.

"I guess I'm just not that memorable!" I laugh, before gulping down some wine in the hope my nerves will settle.

Derek flashes an all-knowing grin like a cat about to catch a mouse. "I see."

My legs tremble, and my throat dries up.

"Ah, Sally, if you studied there, you would know Professor Willis?" Brady asks me, nudging my foot. The twinkle in his eyes prompts me to take his lead.

"Oh, yes! Professor Willis is amazing! I learned so much from him."

Derek raises a doubtful eyebrow and offers Brady a lop-sided smile. "How do you know a professor from New York, Brady?"

"He's an advisor on a new show I'm working on." Brady turns to me, "I'll tell him I know you."

"Yes—please give him my regards," I say, smiling ear to ear, thankful I've been saved from the likes of Derek's dark web. But his narrow beady eyes stay riveted on me.

"What is this new show, Brady? Anything exciting?" Madeline asks.

"Sorry, Madeline. I can't say yet. It's top secret," he says, putting his finger to his lips.

Clifford stands up and clears his throat. "If I could have everyone's attention, please."

The dinner table grows quiet. It's not often that Clifford speaks, so when he does it's recognized as important.

"Thank you. I would like to propose a toast. Sean and Sally, may you live a happy and prosperous life together. Sean, you couldn't have chosen a better partner to become part of this family. Your mother and I are very proud of you." He lifts his glass skyward. "To Sean and Sally."

Everyone joins him, with Derek barely making a passable effort. "To Sean and Sally!"

Sean and I share a winning smile while clinking our glasses together.

"Mrs. Maxwell," he says with a wide grin.

"Has a nice ring to it, don't you think?" I reply before joining in some celebratory chatter across the table with Madeline. Sean leans across behind me to Brady, and I hear him whisper.

"Who's Professor Willis?"

"Have no idea," Brady whispers back before awarding me a huge fake smile that ironically makes me trust him.

Sean and I jump up and down like children high on a sugar rush. "We did it!" We collapse side by side on the bed and giggle with satisfaction and relief.

I turn my head to him. "You'll be CEO!"

Sean turns to me. "And you'll be able to leave your shitty job!"

Immediately my smile dissolves, and I turn my head to look at the ceiling.

"I'm sorry, I thought that's what you wanted?" he says.

My voice softens. "It is. It's just … while playing happy families with you, I forgot about my *other* life for a moment. It's not all bad. It's an honest job. Everyone needs groceries, right?"

"And people like me need a place to sell to. I appreciate everyone who works at a grocery store," Sean says gently. I can tell he's trying to make up for his degrading comment.

I offer him a kind smile, and he tangles our fingers together before letting our joined hands fall to the bed. "I've never seen someone as gorgeous as you working at one though."

The heat between us sparks a current of electricity that casts an unshakable spell over me. From the firm grip of his hand and his teasing eyes I know he can feel it too, and this realization causes my rational mind to malfunction.

"If you were my real fiancée right now, I'd kiss you," he says, his tone low and intimate.

"What are you waiting for?" I reply softly.

His eyes crinkle at the edges, and the corner of his lips curl upwards. He places his hand around my waist, pulling me in. Then he gently brushes his soft lips over mine. I know it's reckless to give in to this feeling. Our time is coming to an end. But I have never felt intoxicating passion like this with anyone before. Something deep inside me rearranges itself while he kisses me.

"Right!" Madeline barges into the room, and Sean tears himself away from me. I clamp my hand over my mouth in embarrassment.

"Mom!" Sean exclaims.

"Now, now. No more hanky-panky until you're married!" Madeline links her arm through mine. "Come on, Sally, off you go. You know it's bad luck to sleep in the same room the night before a wedding. Grab your things. You're sleeping in the guest room tonight."

Sean crosses his arms and taps his foot, watching me retrieve my things in a frenzy. I give him a rueful smile as Madeline hurries me out of the room.

"See you on the other side?" I implore, suddenly feeling hesitant.

Sean sends me a reassuring look. "I'll be there."

Derek

· ❤ · ❤ · ❤ · ❤ · ❤ ·

"Can you stop doing that, Derek? You're making me nervous," Victoria snaps.

I stop my ferocious pacing and rub my eyebrows. "Something is still not right. I can feel it."

"Derek, why can't you just let him be happy? Is it because you're not?" Vic asks, putting her phone down in her lap.

"I know this is just a stunt so he can weasel his way into a partnership. Who does he think he is? I'm the eldest, not him!"

"A three-year age gap isn't much. And *so what?* You might need Sean more than you need the extra money. Then maybe you'll have extra time to spend with Katie and me. This sibling rivalry you have with him must stop!"

I snort and sit on the bed, not wanting to admit I've been a terrible husband. "I guess they do look good together," I say reluctantly as my mouth curls into an aggrieved scowl.

"That's more like it." Vic continues to watch her video and gush over the latest runway trends she insists on draping herself in. Then her head jolts back in irritation. "Ahh!"

"What is it?" I ask.

"Oh, nothing. I just hate ads."

Victoria laughs, and from her phone, I hear a phony French accent declare, *"All I want is a-penis!"*

"What will they come up with next," she says, shaking her head.

"What's so funny?"

"Can you believe this! Who would want to buy these condoms after watching a ridiculous commercial like this?"

I grab the phone from her and take a closer look. My eyes zero in on the screen like darts finding the bullseye, and I look back at Victoria in astonishment.

"Nooo!"

"What in the world, Derek?"

I look to the ceiling in disbelief. I need to watch it again to be certain, so I google 'weird medieval condom commercial.'

I play the clip again and watch the actress wave her delicate handkerchief from a balcony at the groveling knights in shining armor below her. A knight takes a step forward. *"I can give you all the"*—he winks—*"happiness you desire, my lady."* The actress gasps and lets go of her handkerchief which the knights fight each other to catch.

Then the commercial cuts to the actress wearing a giant condom over her head while holding a packet of condoms next to her face. She shoots a Dr Evil look directly into the camera.

"Condomees, where the future of pleasure is at the"—tilts her head meaningfully—*"head of its game."*

I pause the video just after the actress tilts her head, giving me a good look into her sultry eyes. Then I zoom in and study her face like I'm on a treasure hunt. "Holy mackerel!!"

"Derek, what is it?"

I stare at the wall before me, grinning. Slowly, I pass the phone to Victoria. "Look like anyone you know?"

Victoria swipes her phone from my hands. "Derek, why would I know this girl? She's awful."

"Look past the condom on her head," I say, enjoying seeing Victoria's face transform into a look of bamboozlement. She gasps and claps a hand over her mouth. She stares at me with wide, astonished eyes and I feel like I have just won the lottery.

"It *can't* be," Vic splutters.

"BINGO!"

Chapter 22

Sean

I GLANCE AT MY watch. It's just past midnight, and all I can think about is Sal. Is she still awake? I stand at the window in my boxer shorts, staring at the full moon. I tap my forefinger repetitively against my lip. After restless pacing, I force myself into bed and draw the covers up over my face. Not even a minute goes by before I throw the covers off and sit upright, panting like I'm running out of air.

I head to the door and gently open it. I stare down the long dark hallway and size up Sal's door. *Fuck it.* I make my way through the dark, taking light steps, wondering if I'm about to make a massive fool of myself. But my urge to see her trumps any logical thoughts I might be having. A few steps away from her door, the floor creaks loudly beneath my bare foot. I cement my eyes shut and freeze like a Greek statue, praying no one heard.

Sal

The luminous moon mesmerizes my dreamy eyes and I entertain the thought of sneaking into Sean's room. My mind tells
me it's an absurd idea, but my heart urges otherwise. Being a
firm believer in following your heart, I disobey what's left of
my rational mind and palm the bedroom door handle. The
latch makes a sharp *click*, terrifying me, and I abort my silly
plan. I lean against the door helplessly, pining for more of his
touch. With a sigh, I glide toward my bed, but stop as there's
a sound outside my door.

A surge of adrenaline floods my veins at the thought of him
being close. I listen intently for any other sounds. But all I hear
are the voices in my head telling me I'm crazy. Then a loud
creak hooks my attention and I fling myself around to look at
the door. My heart races with the knowledge that this is not
just in my head, so I fearlessly stride to the door. When I pull
it open, Sean's eyes fly open too.

His raw smoldering gaze says everything I need to know. I
look at him through lowered lashes, luring him into the room
with teasing eyes. As soon as the door clicks, he spins me
toward him. His hands are on my lower back, and our eyes lock
before he tastes my lips. I'm enchanted by the light breeze of his
breath and the electric charge zapping between us. The moon
shines more brightly, and so do his eyes as he stares into my
soul. There's no escaping his hungry touch, but I don't want
to. I run my fingernails gently over his bare chest and melt into
him. He easily lifts me so my legs wrap around his hips then
kisses me with a passion I have never experienced before.

The morning sun shines upon my face as I wake. I smell Sean's
scent on the pillow and smile at memories of his gentle yet

masculine touch and electrifying kisses. I reach for my phone, six am. Next to the phone is a note:

Happy Birthday Wifey

I hold the note close to my chest and squeal with joy. No man I've dated has ever remembered my birthday, let alone referred to me as *wifey*.

Cue the wedding bells!

I leap out of bed and dance in my underwear, admiring the birds frolicking outside the window. *I'm getting married today!*

I'm face to face with the—*my*—wedding dress as it hangs from the curtain rail in a downstairs guest room. Butterflies emerge from the pit of my belly.

"Knock, knock!"

I open the door in my white silk robe and welcome Madeline, who has a perplexed expression on her face.

"Something wrong, Madeline?"

Madeline lowers her voice. "Sally, I thought you said your makeup artist was a man?"

Instantly I'm confused. "Yes, he is."

"Then who is this?" Madeline opens the door wide and Carlos screams in excitement, throwing his hands in the air.

"Surprise, Sal!"

My eyes grow wide at the sight of the dark brown tresses that fall to the middle of his back. He is rocking a bright purple faux-fur coat, chunky boots and extravagant makeup that's giving 'pop star on tour.'

"Carlos?"

"Yes bitch! Do you love or do you *love!?*"

"Obviously I love! I'm so happy for you. You look amazing!"

"Thanks. But I don't want to outshine you on your big day!" He deposits his giant makeup case on the floor and hugs me while Madeline tries to control her face.

"Very well then, I'll leave you two to it."

"Thanks, Madeline."

"Thank you, Mrs. Maxwell!"

With a dubious nod, Madeline leaves the room. Carlos and I grip each other's arms, jumping up and down.

"Holy shit, you're getting married today!"

I let go of his arms and inspect his new look. "And *you're* so gorgeous!"

"Don't get too ahead of yourself. I decided I don't want all those hormones you were talking about. Hell to the N-O. But from now on, if I wake up and feel like serving womanly woman that day, I shall do so. Anyone who doesn't like it can suck it!"

"Good for you, Carlos!"

He flamboyantly glides around the room, glowing with relish. "Chica, if this is their holiday home, I'd love to see their real home. This is sick!"

"Isn't it insane?"

Carlos brushes my wedding dress with his hand. "What's *insane* is this nutty thing. Please tell me this isn't your dress!"

I shrug my shoulders helplessly. "Umm ..."

"Have no fear. Carlos is here! I'll just have to make sure your hair and makeup are on point!"

"I was hoping you'd say that."

"But only if you fill me in on all the gossip," he says, pulling out a chair next to the vanity mirror. "Sit down, chica, I'll make a bride of you yet!"

"Carlos, I can't breathe," I pant in a broken voice.

"Just hold it there," he replies, finally getting the zip to the top of my dress. "Mission complete!"

I release a sigh of relief. Carlos fusses over my dress from all angles before stepping back. *"Preciosa!"*

"Huh?"

"You look beautiful, Sal," he says, guiding me toward the full-length mirror. I take a deep breath and step forward. Tingles speed up my body, and tears fill my eyes. Small white flowers are weaved through my low bridal bun. My makeup is flawless with a pop of red lipstick. The diamond tear-drop earrings Madeline let me borrow complement the off-the-shoulder poufy dress.

"Not bad, huh?" he says.

Overwhelmed with gratitude, I embrace him and start to cry on his shoulder.

"Uh-uh, Sal, save the tears for later. We are *not* doing your makeup again."

"I just wish this was real. Then at least Fran, Piper and my parents could be here."

"It will be real one day. But for now, get the bag and move on." He arches an eyebrow and continues, "Unless that's not what you want?"

I pout. "He's sweeter than I thought. He's so down to earth. And his smile—"

Carlos brashly interrupts me. "Mother of God, please don't tell me you slept with him?"

Before I have the chance to respond, I hear Madeline outside my door. "Are we decent in there Sally?"

I flash Carlos a cheeky wink, then call, "Come in!"

Madeline cautiously walks into the room dressed in a teal V-neck lace dress accented with fine jewelry. She gasps, throwing her arms around me. "I can't wait to see Sean's face when he sets eyes on you."

"Thanks, Madeline. You were right. The dress fits perfectly."

"There's just one thing missing," Madeline says, smiling.

I give Carlos a suspicious look, wondering what it could be.

"You can come in!" Madeline exclaims in a loud cheerful voice.

The door flings open, and so does my mouth when Fran and Piper dance their way into the room, stunning in matching sparkly pink dresses. "We're *he-re!*" Fran sings.

Madeline flashes a pleased smile like she's done me a favor and leaves the room.

"What are you two doing here?!" I ask, feeling the blood rush to my head.

"Ah ... not the welcoming response I thought we'd get! You didn't think we'd miss our best friend's wedding, did you?" Piper says, joining in on a three-way hug with Fran. The smothering hug forces me to speak.

"Guys, I know you're excited, but I can't breathe."

Fran and Piper pull back and look at me.

"You look stunning, Sal! Not the dress I thought you would choose, but I adore it on you," Piper says.

Fran shows her softer side. "Yeah, girl. That Sean fella is one lucky man."

I look at Carlos standing in the corner of the room, and I can tell he's entertained by this disastrous situation.

"Sorry! You must be Carlos!" Fran exclaims, approaching him.

He toys with his hair. "That would be me."

"I'm loving the hair!" Fran says with enthusiasm.

Carlos flicks his hair behind his shoulder and pouts his lips. I smile, knowing he's enjoying the attention. "Thanks."

"Nice to meet you, Carlos. We've heard a lot about you," Piper says, extending her hand.

He glances at me. "Only some of it is true."

He flings Piper's hand away and gives her a hug, making her laugh.

I clear my throat. "Um, what are you guys doing here?"

"Girl! Do you think we'd miss the event of the year?" Fran exclaims before Piper cuts in.

"We were going to tell you. It was so painful not speaking for a whole week, but when Madeline got in touch with *Brides and Beauty* I knew exactly where to come. So, we thought we'd surprise you! *Surprise!*"

I raise my palms in the air and lower my voice. "Wait! Why did Madeline contact *Brides and Beauty?*"

"Well, duh. So we can do a feature on your wedding! You're making the front cover! Happy birthday to you!"

"What!" My voice elevates. "Photographers are here?"

"The whole shebang! I made sure your wedding day will get the attention it deserves. You only get married once, and although we think it's rushed, if you love him then who are we to judge? Love shouldn't be bound by time."

My insides feel like they are going to explode. The top half of my body withers over and I take refuge by the window. I realize I can't inhale enough air.

Confusion crosses Piper's dolled-up face. Carlos bites his lower lip, and Fran rubs my back. "Sal, you're not going to die on your wedding day, are you?"

"Um, honey, we have one more surprise," Piper says faintly.

I turn my reddened face to her. "No! No more surprises. *I hate surprises!*"

"Do you really think we could keep this a secret from your parents, Sal?" Fran asks.

An alarmed sound like I've been kicked in the stomach escapes me. My thumping heart drops to the floor. My voice comes out very small. "My parents are here?"

"Don't worry, girl. We filled them in, and they're not angry—a little confused. But Sal, they're happy for you. You have nothing to worry about."

I launch at Fran, grabbing her arms. "Where are they?!"

Fran steps back. "Relax, they're just talking to your new in-laws."

"No!" I cry, rushing out the door.

Chapter 23

Sal

BURSTING INTO THE LIVING room like a flustered bridezilla, I see my parents talking to Madeline and Clifford.

"Mom! Dad!"

Mom dissolves her conversation with Madeline and looks at me with astonished eyes. I step closer to her as she embraces her heart with her hands and cries, "My daughter's getting married!"

I console her with a hug and offer my dad a weak smile, hoping he receives my mind message telling him *I'm sorry.*

"You should be so proud of your daughter and all her accomplishments," Madeline says.

Mom looks at me in awe before answering. "Yes. We are, aren't we, Barry?"

Dad barely registers what is said as he's too busy admiring their luxurious house. Mom nudges Dad's arm. "Oh, yes. She's done *very* well for herself," Dad mumbles, smiling at me when he should be scowling instead.

Clifford addresses Dad. "Barry, you must be happy that Sally's living in LA again?"

I cut in at razor-blade speed, looking at the clock. "Ah, look at the time. I better finish getting ready. Mom, Dad—care to join me?"

"Go ahead. We must greet our guests soon anyway. But I want to know all about our new family after the ceremony!" Madeline says.

I smile politely at Madeline and Clifford before swiftly taking my parents' hands and guiding them to my dressing room.

"What did you tell them?" I demand, eyeballing my parents.

Mom shoots Dad a questioning look before answering. "Nothing, sweetheart."

Relieved, my muscles relax, and I smile. I look around at the baffled stares from every person in the room except Carlos. "Mom, Dad. I'm sorry I didn't tell you."

Mom looks at me with kindness. "Sal, I knew you were dating someone. It hurts me to think you couldn't tell your own mother you were getting married."

Dad chimes in. "Sal, if this is what you want, then let's do it! You're not getting any younger, and it looks like you chose well."

Mom whacks him on his chest. "Quiet, Barry! They could hear you."

"What? We don't have to pay for a wedding. Do you know how much money this saves us, Beth?!"

Carlos, Fran, and Piper are huddled together giggling. I clap my hands together. "Okay, everyone out!"

Bewildered eyes turn to me. "I'm sorry. I love it that you're all here. I just need a moment to myself."

"Of course, dear," Mom says, kissing me on the forehead. "I'm so proud of you."

Dad takes her arm and gives me a fleeting wink before they leave the room along with Fran and Piper, who offer me reassuring smiles.

"Will you be alright, Sal?" Carlos gently asks.

I reluctantly nod. "Carlos?"

"Yeah?"

"Make sure people don't get too close out there. If you know what I mean?"

He gives me a military-style salute and leaves the room.

Sean

"You *what?!*"

"Chill out, Brady. It's no big deal," I say, putting on my tie in front of a full-length mirror.

"I knew it!"

"Knew what?"

"That you're in love with her."

I laugh his comment off and ignore the tingling sensations in my stomach when I think about her. I try my hardest to suppress the flashbacks of Sal kissing my neck, which evoke sensations I do not want to entertain.

"Well, how was it?" Brady asks.

"It was nice."

Brady mocks my casual tone. "*It was nice.* Sheesh, you sound like you're complimenting a meal from Taco Bell!"

I turn to face him. "I'm not sure about this tie?"

"I like it. You can't go wrong with white," Brady replies.

I turn back to the mirror and loosen up my shoulders. But I know I can't properly relax until the day is over.

Brady meets my eyes in the mirror. "Well?"

I turn around again. "It was amazing! You happy now?"

Brady collides his hands triumphantly and spins around laughing. "This is too good!"

"What can I say? She makes me feel fantastic. She's fun, kind and smart. I've never met anyone like her." I smile. "And those eyes."

"Ah, man. You've got it bad, ah?"

I chuckle and extend my wrists, signaling Brady to put the cuff links on.

"I bet you can't wait to see what she looks like?"

"I'm sure she'll look stunning," I say.

Brady adjusts the cuff links. "There we are. You're all set."

"Cheers," I respond, knowing that before the hour is up, I'll be a married man and the CEO position will be in the bag. I straighten my tuxedo and turn to Brady. "Here I go."

Brady stops me from walking out the door. "As your groomsman, it's my duty to ask. Are you sure you want to go through with this?"

I place a reassuring hand on his shoulder. "I've never been more certain of anything."

Sal

·❤·❤·❤·❤·❤·

"This wedding is going to go really well."
"This wedding is going to go really well."
"This wedding—"

My affirmations are suspended by a knock at the door. I turn away from the mirror and yell, "Not now!"

A moment passes, and the door gently opens. My worried expression softens as Derek enters the room. "Oh. Sorry, Derek. I thought you were someone else."

"Your parents and friends are mingling with the other guests if that's whom you're referring to?"

I zip my head back toward the mirror and gulp in fear that my true identity will slip out. But I'm comforted knowing Carlos will be holding court with his charisma amped up to ten, hopefully deterring any leaks.

"You look a bit stressed for someone about to get married," Derek observes.

"It's all a bit overwhelming, that's all. I am happy. Truly."

His eyes linger over my decolletage. "You certainly scrub up well."

"It's your mom's dress."

"I know. All she could go on about was how wonderful it is that you're wearing her dress!" He crosses his arms and puts his finger to his chin. "Gosh, it would truly break her heart if this didn't work out."

"Lucky for her, it's going to work out," I say, clenching my fists. "I'd better finish getting ready, Derek. I'll be out in a moment."

"I just came to wish you luck."

"Thank you."

I thought he would get the hint and leave. Instead, he invades my space even more and a heavy feeling in my stomach anchors me to my chair.

He continues. "And to show you ... this!" He pulls out his phone and taps play. The moment I see myself on screen promoting cheap condoms, my hands tremble with fear and my heart shatters into a million pieces.

He circles me like I'm a deer in the wild about to be shot. "Sally Williams, hmm? Or is it Sally Gardner? An actress from—"

"Stop!" I rise from my chair and meet his manipulating eyes. "What do you want?"

He speaks directly into my ear in a quietly intense voice, making me shudder. "I don't know what game you think you're playing, but I want you to leave my family alone."

My body weakens, and tears stream down my flushed cheeks. "I'm sorry. It wasn't meant to be like this."

"Either you call the wedding off, or everyone will see"—he shoves his phone right in my face—"this!"

I can't speak through my blubbering cry. I watch him leave, along with my hopes for a new life and a man I have grown to love. The thought of Sean's disappointment, along with that of both our families, crumbles my heart into dust.

Thump, thump, thump is the only sound I hear as my heart thrashes wildly against my chest. Nervously, I wait on the deck behind a white curtain and anticipate the music that's my cue for what may be the most disastrous scene of my life.

Fran and Piper rub my arms and tell me they love me before taking their place on the front line.

Dad taps me on the shoulder. "Everything okay, Sal?"

"Yeah, Dad, I'm fine."

Katie tugs on my dress. I crouch down and hold her hand.

"You're the prettiest bride I've ever seen."

"You're the prettiest flower girl *I* have ever seen." I touch her cheek, and the traditional *Bridal Chorus* song starts to play. I link my arm with Dad's as I let out a slow breath and a terrified tear. Fran and Piper peek back at me and smile. There's nowhere to hide. My only hope is for Derek to change his evil mind. How can someone have the heart to destroy lives right before a wedding? *Could he be bluffing?*

Katie looks behind her for confirmation to go ahead. I put on an encouraging smile and give her a thumbs up. Dad looks down at the bouquet of white roses trembling in my clammy hands.

"You sure you're okay, kiddo?"

"Dad, I don't think I can do this."

"It's normal to get cold feet, Sal. Just breathe."

"No, Dad I—"

"Do you love him?"

I ponder before answering, "Yes, I think I do."

"Then let's go."

I unlink my arm from his. "No, you see, that's the problem!"

He gently threads his arm back through mine and nudges forward, but I dig my heels into the red carpet, unwilling to budge.

"Come on, dear! Let's not keep our guests waiting," Dad says through gritted teeth before nudging me harder, propelling me through the curtain and into the spotlight.

My face scrunches up, bewildered by the blinding bright flashes that shine from numerous photographers, from every direction. I plaster on a fake smile and follow Dad's lead down the red-carpeted aisle. We pass what seems like hundreds of people adorned in couture, black bowties and colorful headpieces.

I hear gasps and whispers, and animated eyes watch my every step. But as I look ahead, the only eyes I see are Sean's.

His stance is confident and relaxed but the intensity of his gaze tells me he's nervous too. He looks ravishing in his tuxedo and the closer I get to him, the brighter his smile shines. He looks just like Ken but way better. Like, waaay better. *Cue the heart-flutters*. I offer Mom and Carlos a slight nod and tiny smile as I walk past them. Then Dad hands me over to Sean with a firm handshake. "Look after my daughter, will you," Dad says.

Sean gives him a reassuring smile, and I can tell from his eyes that he wasn't expecting to meet Dad. "You look beautiful," Sean whispers.

"So do you," I reply. "I mean, handsome, you look handsome." We share a nervous giggle, and the music stops.

Through the silence, I hear an abrupt throat being cleared. From the corner of my eye, I see Derek tapping his phone, standing next to Madeline and Clifford, who are already shedding tears of joy.

"You may all be seated," the marriage officiant says, looking like she's dressed for a funeral instead of a wedding.

My hands tremble in Sean's. "Just look at me," he whispers.

But my eyes keep cutting to Derek, who raises his eyebrows every time I look at him. The officiant gives a speech about the meaning of love that washes right over me. I'm too busy thinking about escape plans and praying a UFO will crash-land on Derek.

"Sean, do you take Sally to be your wife, to have and to hold from this day forward, for richer, for poorer, in sickness and in health, to love and to cherish until death do you part?"

"I do." His voice is strong and determined.

A whirlwind of emotion engulfs me as I look into Sean's eyes. A part of me wants to go through with it, but the risk of Derek exposing my fraud via that horrendous condom commercial is too high. I can feel my pulse throbbing in my wrist. It's time I take matters into my own hands, but I don't know how.

"Sally, do you take Sean's hand in—"

"I ... I ..."

The officiant clears her throat. "Excuse me. I'm not finished yet."

"Sorry," I reply. As she proceeds, my eyes dance around everyone looking at me, including my mom, who tightly grips Dad's hand. Fran and Piper wipe away tears, and I see Carlos perched on the edge of his seat sending me an encouraging look. Little Katie giggles with excitement on Victoria's lap, but Derek is shooting daggers at me with his demon eyes. I look at Sean and feel unbearable sorrow as I helplessly let go of his hands.

He gently shakes his head as if he knows what I'm about to do. "Sally."

"I'm sorry," I whisper.

"Stop. Please." He lowers his tone. "I've fallen in love with you."

Those words ambush me with a profound wave of joy like nothing I've ever felt before. My heart feels like it's going to explode. I close my eyes, and tears stream down my face. I open my eyes and take a breath that will be my last as a respected fiancée, doctor, friend and daughter.

"Then I hope you can forgive me," I say.

I signal the marriage officiant to stop talking and address the crowd. In particular, Madeline and Clifford, who continue to smile brightly even though I know they can tell something's not right.

"I came here today to marry your son—your amazing son—for ..."

Sean grips my wrist. "Don't do it, Sal." But regretfully I ignore him, and proceed.

"For *money*."

A sound like a crying cat shrieks out of Madeline. Gasps ripple through the guests. I try not to look at Fran and Piper's aghast faces and ignore Carlos's death stare telling me to stop.

The photographers come in closer, flashing away as I continue. "I am not a doctor. I'm just an unemployed actress working as a checkout girl."

Shocked eyes and whispers behind hands are everywhere I look. Clifford rises from his chair. "But Sally, you saved me!"

"I'm sorry, Clifford. That was a total fluke," I explain, directing an apologetic look at Madeline.

"I can't cook to save myself, I shop at Walmart, and I don't eat meat."

Brady hides his head in the lapel of his tuxedo, but I hear him murmur under his breath. "Oh man, this is *good*."

Clifford and Madeline make horrifying sobbing sounds while holding onto each other. Victoria comforts them while seeing Derek leap from his chair. "See. Told ya! I knew she was a fake fraud!"

As his words render me to the floor, Victoria stands tall. "Derek. I want a divorce!" Katie's whimpering cry seeps through the cold silence. Victoria plasters on a phony smile, ironing out her dress with her hands. "Did I just say that out loud?" She sits next to Katie and whispers that she didn't mean it. Derek and his ego march away from the venue.

Mom and Dad watch me in complete disbelief, and I'm afraid I've disappointed them again.

I get up off my knees and gaze upon Madeline and Clifford, who look like they are on the verge of needing a real doctor. *How could I let this happen?* "The truth is, I thought I could gain your approval by being someone I'm not so that you would accept me as Sean's bride. I don't know *who* I am anymore. But I do know what I want."

I turn to Sean, who looks back at me through his splayed fingers, chin close to his chest. His gentle eyes bore into me with a heavy sadness that I wish I hadn't caused.

"So, it *is* true!" Everyone follows a high-pitched voice to the back of the tent, where a tall blonde stands in a short red minidress that reveals her busty boobs.

Sean's eyes cut to me before returning to the woman in red. "Monica?"

"Monica?" I mutter. Why does she seem so familiar?

As Monica struts her way down the aisle like she owns the place, I realize she's the model from Veronica's agency. I grimace and brace myself as she approaches me.

Monica points her long finger at me. "You?! What's a sad sight like you doing here?"

Madeline steps in. "Excuse me, and you are?"

"I'm his girlfriend!"

The crowd gasps loudly, and Sean rubs his temples. "*Ex*-girlfriend."

I take a good look at Sean, knowing this might be the last time I see him. Then I give Madeline my most apologetic look. With all the dignity I have left I flee down the aisle through the gossiping crowd, blinking back my tears.

Sean

I try to catch Sal's attention through the flashes and eruption of the rowdy crowd, but a sudden slap across the face from Monica throws me off course. "You pig!"

Mom is shaking her head in pure dread. "Why, Sean? Why would you do this to us?!" she babbles hysterically, and a brash photographer steps forward and takes a picture of her. "No more photos! Everybody out!" she screams.

I can't believe, at a time like this, Brady is trying to chat up one of Sal's bridesmaids. But she ignores him, ruffles up her dress and grabs the other bridesmaid's hand. They both run after Sal, along with her parents. Someone who looks like her roommate dressed as a woman excuses himself with a theatrical bow.

Amidst the chaos, I follow them through the gossiping crowd and run to our room. Her suitcase is gone. All that's left is the wedding dress on the bed with the diamond ring beside it. No note, no goodbye. The show is over.

Chapter 24

Sal

I ROLL MY LUGGAGE into my apartment with the help of my parents after a gloomy and depressing flight back to LA. The only sign of a smile from me is when I see Oscar wagging his tail. "Someday, huh, Oscar."

Mom and Dad loiter aimlessly. I see them observe a cockroach race across the peeling paint on my walls, which I admit I have let deteriorate since they last visited me over a year ago.

"Sal, I don't understand. We would have given you money if that's what you needed," Dad says.

"Your father's right. We have a little bit of savings that we can spare."

"I wanted to do it on my own. I'm thirty now, Mom, and I can't even support myself!"

"So, you pretended to be a doctor and a fiancée to the son of a rich family? Do you know how strange that is?!" Mom's tone is infused with a passion I haven't heard since I was caught with a cigarette in my teens.

Fran, Piper, and Carlos barge through the door, chatting like besties but stop abruptly when they see Mom's reddening face. "We can come back?" Carlos offers.

Agonizing defeat splatters all over my face. In an ashamed tone, I respond. "No, please stay."

Mom's face softens as she throws an arm around me. "Sal, you may have had a rough ride lately, but just because you aren't where you think you should be in life doesn't mean you're worthless."

Fran places her bag on the kitchen bench and approaches me. "Your mom's right. If you weren't fabulous, we wouldn't be friends!"

"Ditto on that one," Piper says, high-fiving Fran.

"Look around, guys. This is my life. Pretending to be Sean's fiancée as well as a doctor was exhilarating. I felt like I was *someone*, someone that I could be proud of."

"We're all proud of you, Sal," Dad says, watching my eyes fill with tears. "Did you mean what you said about this man Sean before we walked down the aisle?"

I regard him through watering eyes and nod. Troubled looks fill the room, and I can tell they feel sorry for me. I'm the one who put myself here. *I'm* the one who should be sorry.

Everyone huddles around me, hugging me until I stop crying. "Okay, okay, guys. Enough with the mushy stuff! I'm fine. You can all go home now. Except for you, Carlos, but only because you live here."

"And leave you alone on your birthday? No way, girlfriend," Fran declares, placing a hand on her hip.

"Gosh, I wish we had some wine right now," Piper mutters.

Carlos smiles like the Cheshire Cat and grabs two bottles of Moet out of his bag and parades them in the air like they're Emmy Awards. "Well, lucky for you guys, I'm here!"

"Oh my gosh, did you pinch them from the wedding?" I say with wide eyes.

He shrugs his shoulders. "Alright, chica, I don't think you're in a position to judge," he laughs. "Plus they had hundreds of bottles just going to waste. You damn well earned these, Sal. Tonight, we celebrate your birthday!"

Sean

I hear plates and wine glasses crashing onto the deck from where I sit at the kitchen island nursing my glass of whiskey. Suddenly the air grows cold as Mom stomps through the kitchen in her high heels, carrying broken plates. Dad soon follows. He calmly places a hand on Mom's shoulder. "Feeling better now, darling?" he asks.

Mom flares her nostrils, clenches her fists, and glares out the window at the sight of the dismantled party. Dad sits down on a wooden stool opposite me. "You on the drink again, son?"

"What do you care, Dad? And I'm not an alcoholic. I screwed up for *one* night. If you didn't demote me and treat Derek like such a god, then maybe we wouldn't be here."

"I see," Dad responds, raising an eyebrow.

Mom whips her head around to me, giving me a murderous stare. "Oh, so it's our fault now, Sean? Do you know what this will do to the business? *Do you?*"

I bite my tongue in an effort not to respond. I know an impulsive reaction will only make matters worse. Instead, I take another sip of whiskey.

"Well, Clifford! Did you see the look on our friend's faces? We are ruined!"

I shake my head, not able to suppress my feelings any longer. "Don't flatter yourself, Mom. We're not as big as you think.

No one will care in two weeks. Besides, do you think your 'friends' would still be around if you didn't have money?" I demand, looking at her. She's near tears, which makes me instantly regret my words.

"I'm sorry for what I've put you through, I don't know what I was thinking. But although my relationship with Sal wasn't real, it was still more real than any of this!"

"What's got into you?!" Mom barks.

"I love her, Mom!" I reply without thinking twice.

The sudden creak of a wooden floorboard sounds loudly through the eerie silence.

"I'll never forgive you for this, Sean!" Mom spits in rage, storming out of the kitchen.

"I'm not surprised, son," Dad says, and a sorrowful look washes over his face.

"Really?" I ask, raising my head.

"I've seen the way you two look at each other. Love somehow has a funny way of choosing our partners for us."

Dad hardly ever talks about love. He never lets any of us see his softer side. I smile at him as he continues. "The contract is still yours if you want it. I'd be proud to see you sign it."

I freeze, wide-eyed, deep in thought. He still wants me to be CEO? "What? I thought you would disown me after all this?"

"I thought about it. But what good would that do? I'm disappointed, yes, but you obviously wanted the CEO position badly enough to pull off this elaborate stunt."

My voice weakens. "Don't you get it, Dad? All I wanted from you is to see that I could do it *without* all this. I don't care about the money or the status anymore." A realization blooms through me. "In fact, I don't think I want to work for the company at all."

"Don't be ridiculous, son! This company is all you've ever known! What else would you do?"

I cross my arms and smile. "I have an idea."

Sal

A week has passed since I abandoned Sean. Everything has gone back to normal. Instead of making the front page of *Brides and Beauty* magazine, I made the front page of the local paper with the most unflattering image and a headline that read:

Maxwell's Meat Company Ruined by Fake Bride!

I wouldn't have cared so much if I didn't have to sell them at Happy Day Groceries, where people point, stare and laugh at me when they figure out I'm the fake bride. Lucky for me, Helga finds it amusing. It's even bumped up sales. My job is safe. I have a roof over my head and friends and family that care about me. That's more than enough for me.

I walk past Carlos's bedroom and stop to watch as he cheerfully sings and dances with headphones over his ears. I tilt my head back and laugh.

He startles, pulling his headphones down around his neck. "How long have you been standing there?"

"Long enough," I say, with a little wink. "The new you suits you."

I reach into my pocket, pulling a bundle of cash from my pink velvet wallet. "Guess who paid all their rent?"

"What the! How?"

"Turns out people pay top dollar for Gucci!"

"You sold your dresses?"

"They were stunning, but they reminded me of him. Plus, I had enough to get my car back."

"Well, look at you go, chica."

I flash him a bright smile and enter my room. I look at my closet full of miniskirts and tight tops. Although I'm not one to wear high fashion, mainly due to my income, the designer clothes I wore taught me that I deserve the best and that I don't need to dress provocatively to entice men. There is no place for cheap threads in a classy girl's world. However, umm ... I'm not ready to give up *all* the pinks and sparkles just yet.

Pretending to be Sean's fiancée took courage (and a bit of madness), but so did baring my naked face. From now on, I'm only going to wear makeup for *me*.

Bright pink blush, old lipsticks and hair extensions, teeny miniskirts and six-inch heels all get tossed into a trash bag. All that's left are a few items I know Carlos will love.

I tie the bag and survey my room. "All done, Oscar!"

My phone chimes. A jolt of adrenaline rushes through my body. Could it be Sean? I plunge for the phone. Then disappointment crushes the adrenaline as I see it's an unknown number.

Calls from unknown numbers are one of the pains of my life. I have stopped answering them for fear it's either the bank telling me I owe money or it's Ronnie trying to contact me on his mom's phone after I blocked him. I sigh. I am trying to live a less messy life, so here goes.

"Sally speaking."

I listen to the caller on the other end, and my eyes feel like they will pop out. "I didn't expect a call from you," I exclaim.

I proceed to listen with great focus. "Thank you so much! I'll be there," I say before ending the call. I pick up Oscar, twirl him around and screech with excitement.

"Doctor, Doctor. His heart can't take it anymore!" I say in a serious tone, dressed in a set of scrubs.

"Pass me the defibrillator!" Dr. Love exclaims.

Dr. Love buzzes the patient's chest with the paddles. "He's not going to make it."

"Give me that!" I say, pushing Dr. Love out of the way. "Don't die on me today, sonny." After using the defibrillator, I perform a round of chest compressions. Then the patient shows signs of life.

"You saved him, Dr. Walker."

"*We* saved him, Dr. Love," I say.

I hold an intense gaze until I hear the words, "And *CUT!*"

"Thank you, Sally," Brady says, giving the casting director a nod before smiling at me. "I think we got what we needed."

"Are you sure? I can try it with a bit more subtlety?"

"No, Sally. You took that direction perfectly. If you get the role, you'll hear back from us within the week."

"Thanks, Brady," I say, hoping I did enough to book a lead role on my favorite series, *Dr. Love*.

Brady chases me into the parking lot. "Hey, have you heard from him yet?" he asks, no longer in professional mode.

I allow him a weak smile, shaking my head. "Why would he want to speak to me after what I did?"

"I know when my best friend likes a girl. How do you think I got your number?"

"How's he doing?" I ask, my smile widening.

"Why don't you ask him yourself?"

I bite my lip, trying not to seem too excited at the thought of seeing Sean again. "Thanks, Brady."

I turn away from him, and let a huge smile take over my face.

Chapter 25

Sean

SCRATCHING MY HEAD IN deep contemplation, I look over a spread of photographs of wild animals. I lean back in my chair and smile. I grab my camera and scroll through my latest images, then stop at a photo of Sal on our hike.

A knock on the door breaks me out of my indulgent thoughts. Immediately I spring from my chair in the ridiculous hope that it might be Sal. For probably the tenth time today, I thought about how she was doing. I struggle to forget how she made me feel when she was in my arms. Brushing crumbs off my jeans from toast and peanut butter, I open the door.

"Hungry?" Monica asks, holding two muffins in front of her chest, dressed in a red trench coat.

My eyes dim and I cross my arms. "I've eaten."

"I bet you haven't had dessert."

"Monica, what do you want?"

"I came to say I'm sorry."

"Great, you've said it. You can go." As I push the door closed, Monica pushes back and makes her way past me into my living area.

"Monica, I'm kind of busy right now."

She unbuttons her trench coat which I watch fall to my marble floor. My gaze travels up her long tanned legs and past her red lace underwear.

"Too busy for this?" She pouts her enhanced lips.

I bite my bottom lip. She was visually beautiful, I'll give her that. I used to find her hard to resist, but now I feel nothing.

"Excuse me! A half-naked girl is offering herself to you, and you just stand there?" Monica says, waving long fingers in front of my face.

"Monica, it was fun what we had. But we broke up for a reason. I've moved on."

She steps closer, drawing circles on my white T-shirt with her finger.

"Come on. I'm back for the week. Thought we could have some fun." The teasing seduction in her voice is more than a little tempting. I try to hold it together as her finger travels toward my belt.

"If by 'moving on' you mean that trainwreck of a wannabe-fiancée, then I'm a little worried about your mental health."

I brush her hand away and step back. "Leave her out of this!"

A faint knocking comes through the door. I cock my head, unsure who it could be. I extend my palms to Monica. "Don't move."

"I'm not going anywhere, cowboy."

I look through the peephole. My pulse takes off at the sight of Sal twisting her hair around her fingers. *"Shit!"*

"Who is it, hot stuff?" Monica asks.

I run to Monica and pick her coat up off the floor. "Quickly, put this back on." I lead her to my bedroom and squeeze her hot body into my closet.

"What are we doing, Sean?"

"Please be quiet. Do *NOT* come out until I say so."

I run to the front door and catch Sal's attention just before the elevator door opens.

"Sal?!"

Sal refrains from hopping into the elevator. "Hi, Sean."

I drink her in, my yearning for her is stronger than ever. My grin is huge, I couldn't wipe it off if I tried.

Sal glides over to me. "So, you do live here."

"Yep, at least that part wasn't a lie."

"Sorry to come unannounced. I was just in the neighborhood and—"

"No, I'm glad you came."

I look behind to make sure there is no sign of Monica.

"I'm sorry, are you busy?"

Shoot! How do I deal with this? Of course, she wants to come in. I want her to come in too! I can't risk losing her again. "Um. No. Come in."

"Nice place," Sal says, sweeping her eyes around my living room while I gather empty pizza boxes and hide them in the kitchen. Then I rush to Sal's side, where she lingers at my dining table.

"Sorry. Can I get you anything?"

"No, thank you."

"How have you been?"

"Good. You?"

"Good. Busy."

The elephant in the room puts a tusk-shaped wedge between us, and I want it gone. "I'm sorry I haven't been in touch. I just needed to process everything. But you've been on my mind. Like, a lot."

Sal smiles, stepping toward me. "Stop. Honestly, I don't blame you. I'm the one who broke the deal. Not you."

Her eyes skim the photographs. She looks back at me and grins.

"Have you been taking more photos?"

I push back my hair. "Ah, yeah. I thought it was time I tried something I really want to do."

"Get out of town! This is incredible!"

"You think so? I mean, it's early stages. But I think I can make a go of this."

"Oh my gosh! I'm so proud of you," she says, leaping into my arms. The feel of her warm embrace and the sweet scent of her perfume makes me squeeze her tighter.

"I've missed you," I say softly.

"Sean. I came here to tell you something."

"Go on," I say, looking at her.

"Before I left the altar, you said ..."

I know exactly what I said but wasn't sure she felt the same. "I remember."

"Did you mean it, or did you just say that to get me to stay?"

"What if I did mean it? Would that scare you away?"

"Sean," she says, her tone serious. "I'm in love with you, too."

A rush of heat like I've been lit on fire roars through my body. With tremoring arms, I pull her in tight to kiss her. But I stop just a breath away. Too enthralled by this moment, I have forgotten about Monica who now trots her red heels back into the living room.

"Sorry to break up the love fest! But Sean ... I was getting so cold in your room. I thought you were going to warm me up?"

Monica's half-naked body flashes in Sal's wide eyes. Her jaw gapes, and I feel like the biggest asshole.

"Wow. I can't believe what an idiot I was to imagine this could work," she spits, heading for the door. "Goodbye, Sean. Don't bother contacting me again."

"Sal! You have it all wrong!"

The door slams shut. I turn to Monica and scowl at her.

"Sorry, did I ruin your little reunion?"

"Put your coat on and leave."

Sal

"He did *what?!*" Carlos exclaims.

"I know! I'm not making this up. She just stood there with her fake boobs bursting out of her bra in plain daylight!"

"Shit."

"What the hell was I thinking? I can't believe I thought he loved me."

"Who knows, Sal? Maybe he does."

"Carlos! If you're in love with someone, wouldn't that make you not want to look at other people?"

"I guess so. I don't know. I'm no love expert."

"I rest my case." I whip my phone out and scroll through my numbers.

"Sal, what are you doing?"

"Blocking him. I'm never getting hurt again!" I say, grabbing his business card out of my wallet, ripping it up and tossing it in the trash. I throw myself onto the couch next to Oscar and kick my heels off.

"I'm sorry things didn't work out, Sal."

"Ha! How can anyone fall in love in two weeks? Love is for losers anyway."

He offers me a sorrowful pout as he leaves the room. I huff and open an unread snap from Zac.

Beer?

I scoff at the pathetic and unappealing message but reply anyway.

Still up for that beer?

I watch for his bitmoji peeking up to indicate he received my message. He always replies straight away. And, well, what do ya know! Within seconds a message appears and so does my smile.

Hey, stranger. I'm thirsty. You free now?

In the past, when I'd receive a message from Zac, my excitement level had exceeded a ten. But not this time. Why does this feel so wrong? Still, I betray my instincts and reply.

See you in an hour.

Nervously, I sit in my car outside Zac's house and check my reflection in the mirror. I can't tell if my jitters are from excitement or from stress. I reach for the lipstick and liquid eyeliner in my bag but refrain from putting any on. Instead, I spray some perfume around my neck and pop a mint in my mouth before heading to his front door.

Before I knock, Zac swings the door open like he knew I was already here. He stands in front of me with a beer in his hand, wearing nothing but a towel wrapped around his fine, dark, muscular body. Droplets of water glisten on his skin, and I feel uncomfortable at the way his disoriented whiskey-brown eyes scan my whole body. I know he's not used to seeing me without long hair, dressed in figure-hugging skirts with a full face of makeup.

"Sal?"

"Hi," I reply, sensing his lack of enthusiasm. I wonder if wearing jeans and the Gucci blazer I kept was the right decision.

"You don't look like you. Something's not right."

"I cut my hair and decided it was time for a new look. You like?"

"Ahhh."

The attraction that once sparked so brightly between us fizzles. However, I know Zac's the kind of guy who takes advantage of his good looks and gets a kick out of having his ego stroked by any woman who is willing. He takes a big swig of his beer and invites me inside.

Reluctantly, I follow him to the kitchen, where he hands me a beer. He guides me to the couch in the living room, which is scattered with empty beer bottles and dirty laundry. Feelings of turmoil twirl around the pit of my stomach like a tornado as I watch him press play on the first show he sees on Netflix. I know all too well that watching a movie is the last thing on his mind.

"There we go. I'm all yours now." He leans back on the couch and wraps an arm around my shoulders.

"We're watching a movie?"

"Got any other ideas? I'm sure there are lots of ways we can entertain ourselves," he says, stroking my thigh.

"I thought we could, you know, catch up. I haven't seen you in over a month."

His eyes roll. "Oh yeah. Where have you been? Annabelle misses you." His hand travels up my thigh while his mouth dances above my neck. "I've missed you." Just before his lips touch my skin, I push him away.

"I got fired, Zac. *Fired!*"

"I just thought you must have skipped town or whatever," he says in a cold and arrogant tone.

"Aren't you going to ask me why I got fired?"

He inhales a deep breath and conjures up what seems like a big effort to respond. "Go ahead. Why?"

"Hmm, I suspect the same reason Angela got fired. Do you remember Angela by any chance?"

His eyes widen and he leans back, taking another swig of beer. "I bumped into her a few times. It was nothing serious." He leans into me. "She isn't as cute as you are, though."

He kisses my neck, and although I have dreamed of a guy like Zac jumping all over me like this, my plan to forget Sean is failing and this only makes me think about him more. Flashes of our night together bolt through my mind. The unforgettable scent of his cologne seems to stalk me. All I want is him.

"Stop! What are you doing?" I cry as Zac hauls me on top of him.

"Don't act like you came here to *catch up*. I know you want me, Sal."

I leap off him, laughing sarcastically, before giving him an empty stare. There is no doubt he is a handsome man, but now I can see past the veneer to a sad, insecure man who uses pretty girls to feed his ego.

The awful truth is that perhaps I am no different. I realize I attract these types of men to get a false sense of approval.

But deep down, I never loved myself enough to get the respect I desired from a man. Maybe that's also why I attract the low-paying roles and shitty jobs. It all makes sense now. How can anyone love me if I don't love myself? *It's so simple*, yet it's taken me thirty freaking years to figure this out! *Cue the light bulb!*

I swear to myself that from this point on I will not change who I am to please anyone, I will not base my self-worth on what others think of me. In the words of Carlos, *they can suck it!*

"No, I don't want you, Zac," I say with certainty before fleeing to the front door.

"Just another tease!" he yells.

"Just another LA asshole!"

Zac chases me to the front door, and I quicken my steps to my car.

"Sal! You're nothing but a five … and that was before your little disaster of a make-over!"

Not wanting to give him the satisfaction of seeing my face again, I hold my arm high with my middle finger extended. As soon as I hear his front door slam, I can feel a new door opening for me. The chains of dating men like Zac are broken, and I feel free.

I flip down the top of my yellow convertible and turn up the volume of *You Don't Own Me* by Lesley Gore. With a tight grip on my steering wheel I zoom off and scream out a sound of happiness, letting the cool evening breeze whisk against my skin.

"Thank you, have a happy day!" I repeat, passing a customer their grocery bag.

"Okay, you. Break. Now."

"It's okay, Helga. I'm not hungry."

"Sal, you haven't had a break all day. Go eat something woman! I'm going to have to get you a new uniform. You're disappearing! Is everything alright?"

"Yeah, I'm fine!" I say, but deep down, no matter how hard I try to keep busy, my mind gravitates toward Sean.

Helga taps her foot, waiting for me to leave the checkout.

"I guess I'll go take that break, then."

Sitting on the staffroom couch, I stare at my cold slice of pizza.

"Lost your appetite?" Jeremy asks.

"I can't eat, I can't sleep."

"Sounds like symptoms of love. Well, that's what the movies say."

"Is that what love does? Because if it is, I never want to feel this way again." I slide my pizza across the coffee table to Jeremy. "Have this. I've got to get back to work."

"Thanks! I'm starving."

I feel my phone vibrate through my bag on the way to my locker. I stop mid-step, drop the bag to the floor and rummage through it to find my phone in the hope it's Sean telling me what a big mistake he made. Then I remember I blocked him. Even if I hadn't, I know it would be a mistake to answer after seeing him with another woman. Finally I retrieve my phone. I gasp as my heart speeds up, knowing that the unknown number calling me could be Brady.

"Hello!"

"Sal, Brady here. I've been trying to get hold of you all morning."

"Hi, Brady. Sorry, I'm at work."

"So ..." Brady draws out the suspense while my heart hangs on the line.

"Yes, Brady?"

"You got the role!!"

Draping a hand over my mouth, I weep openly and lower myself the floor. "I can't believe it."

"Believe it. The casting director loved you. Come in and sign contracts, then you start Monday."

Chapter 26

Sal

"CONGRATULATIONS AGAIN, SAL. I'M going to miss you," Jeremy says, locking up the store.

"Thanks, Jeremy. But you still have me for a couple more days."

"You're not going to forget about us when you're famous, are you?"

"Never! I'll come here to get my groceries just to see you."

"Need a ride?"

"No thanks. I've got my car back now and am off to celebrate. I'll see you tomorrow!"

I watch Jeremy ride off on his bike and walk the few steps to my car. I quicken my pace when I notice a shadow lurking behind me. Just before I open my car door, a hand grabs my arm and I scream.

"It's only me, Sally!"

"Derek! You frightened me! What the heck are you doing here?"

"Sorry to scare you," he pauses before he continues. "New job? Sounds exciting."

I raise an eyebrow, then look side to side. Derek continues. "Sorry, I overheard you talking to that boy."

"How did you even know I work here?"

"How do you think?"

"Derek. I did what you asked of me. Now respect my wishes and *leave me alone.*"

"I came here to apologize. Looking back, I could have dealt with the situation differently. But what *you* did was horrendous."

I shrug my shoulders. "I suppose I'm the one who should be sorry."

A weak smile emerges on his face. "I've got to hand it to you. You had us believing you. Mom's still crying over it. I think she genuinely liked you."

"And Clifford? Was he angry after that dreadful feature in the paper?"

"Funny you should ask. Our revenue grew twenty-three percent after that, and there are no signs of it slowing down. Maybe I should be thanking you."

I look down at my feet, happy to hear the good news. "And Victoria?"

"We're um ... we're seeing a shrink."

"Oh. That's great! I thought for a moment I had something to do with it and—"

"Don't flatter yourself, Sally. We haven't been happy for years. Look, I didn't come here to make you feel bad. I came here to tell you that my brother loves you."

"Then why was Monica at his house practically naked?"

"I know it looked bad, but Sean told me she threw herself at him. He told her to leave. There wasn't much to it. I've never seen my brother mope around like such a sad sloth before."

My eyes sparkle, but I stop myself from smiling. "Really?"

"Look, if he's turning away hot girls like that, he's either blind, bats for the other side, or he's in love with someone else."

This is the best news ever, and it's coming from dickhead Derek! Before I let Cupid carry me away, I press him some more. "How do you *know* he loves me?"

"I overheard him tell Mom and Dad."

"Really!? ... Well ... he can tell me himself."

"He said he tried calling you but couldn't get through. Hence yours truly being here."

"He knows where I live. If he actually loves me, he can come and find me." I offer him a firm nod before sliding into my car. "All the best with the company, Derek."

Sean

"Oh, it's *you*," Carlos says with an unimpressed grimace, opening the front door. I quickly scan the living room for any sign of Sal.

"Sorry it's late, Carlos. But is she here?"

"Sean Maxwell ... the nerve! Nope! Sal is not here."

"Do you know when she'll be back?"

"Nope!"

"Look, I know what she's probably told you, but it isn't true."

"Are you calling Sal a liar now?"

"No!" I tilt my head and laugh. "Well, that's debatable really, isn't it?" I can see from Carlos's deadpan stare of hatred he doesn't appreciate my humor.

"I can see how she thought that I was—well," I hesitate, I don't know how to explain why a half-naked woman was in my condo. "Can you please tell her I dropped by so I can explain it to her myself?"

"Oh, sure!" Carlos slams the door in my face before I can thank him.

Sal

On a quieter evening at Tequila Tavern, Fran, Piper, and I clink our glasses in a toast to celebrate my new job.

"Girl, I *cannot believe* you are playing Dr. Love's love interest! Jackpot!" Fran says, sipping her orange juice.

"Me neither." I stare into my cosmo, not even tempted to drink it.

"Sal honey, I thought you'd be happy?" Piper has concern all over her face.

"I am! I am. I just ... when I found out, the first person I wanted to tell was Sean."

"Oh boy," Fran murmurs.

"Sal, why don't you just tell him how you feel?" Piper asks.

"I did, and you know what happened after that."

"Aw, honey," Piper soothes, giving me her classic pity-pat on the back.

"It's okay. I'll get over it." I raise my glass. "Here's to new beginnings. The new me and the friends I can't live without!"

I smooth my Happy Day Groceries uniform with my hands for the last time as I smile at myself in the mirror. I go to the kitchen, where Carlos slurps his cereal.

"Happy last day Sal! You did it!"

"*We* did it, Carlos!"

I scoop some dog food into a bowl, place it on the floor and let out a sigh before resting my arms on the kitchen counter.

"What's wrong, Sal? Shouldn't you be on cloud nine?"

I rest my chin in the palms of my hands. Derek's words were on my mind all night. I can't help but wonder if he was telling the truth. "I just don't understand! If Sean wanted to see me, wouldn't he have tried to contact me?" I stand upright, cross my arms over my chest and screw up one side of my mouth. "I know I blocked him and all. But doesn't true love conquer all?"

Carlos stops the spoonful of cereal from going into his mouth and avoids eye contact.

"What if he *did* try and see you? What would you have done?" he asks.

A joyous smile flashes across my face. I indulge in a moment of fantasy.

"Dreams are free," I shrug. I snap out of my daze and perk up as I retrieve my bag. "But on a more positive note, *some* dreams really do come true!"

I place both hands on Carlos's shoulders. "Carlos, thank you for being there for me. Whether you know it or not, you've changed the way I see myself just by being you. You're not just a roommate but a friend. Hell, one of the girls, even!" I give him a quick embrace and cheerfully head toward the front door. "Wish me luck!"

"Go get 'em, chica. Pack those groceries like it's your last!"

I flash him a smile and a quick curtsy as I skip out the door.

Carlos

My animated smile instantly drops when the door closes behind her. *Shit! What have I done!* I run to the trash to find Sean's business card, but Sal has already taken it to the dumpster. I bolt downstairs and run to the back of the apartment complex.

Before I know it, I'm knee-deep in the putrid stench of garbage bags. *Yuck!* Twenty minutes of relentless searching and fighting my gag reflex because of the slimy sensations touching my hands. The moldy food I try to avoid—spores—ew. I'm about to give up when I spot one piece of the business card under a squashed loaf of bread. A few more minutes of hunting, I find the second half stained with something purple. I put them together and just make out Sean's number.

Man, I'm good! I do a little triumph dance, brush some coffee grounds off the hot pink shirt Sal gave me, and run back upstairs.

My phone is to my ear as I catch my breath, anticipating an answer. It rings, but no one picks up. "What now, Oscar?" I ask, watching Oscar sniff my feet. *Yeah, yeah, I smell, I know.*

I put the phone down on the kitchen counter and go to the bathroom. Then I hear it ringing. Shuffling my steps back to the kitchen like a speed-salsa dancer, I answer.

"Hola?"

"Hi, Sean Maxwell here. I missed a call from this number?"

"Sean. It's me, Carlos!"

"Oh, hey," Sean says, surprised.

"Do you truly love her?"

"Yes. I do, I swear."

"Well, you should probably know it's her last shift at Happy Day Groceries."

"Wait. She got the part?!"

"Ask her yourself."

"I knew she would!"

"If you break her heart, I'll bitch slap you so hard you'll wish you never—"

"Don't worry," he promises, and is gone. I put the phone down and smile with satisfaction. *Mission complete.*

Sal

The clock strikes four and Happy Day Groceries is packed and bustling. But I don't mind, because I'll walk out of here in one hour and start my dream job. I look around the store while I happily pack the customer's groceries. I watch Jeremy laugh, which makes me smile. On the aisle next to his, I see Helga bossing my new replacement around. Although I'm excited to leave, I can't help but feel immense gratitude that Helga took a chance on me.

"Will that be all today, ma'am?" I query, smiling.

The customer nods as I hand over the bag of groceries. "Great, have a happy day!"

My smile quickly dissolves into curiosity when I hear a familiar voice. I glance toward Jeremy's register and see he's serving Fran and Piper, who are giggling like schoolgirls. My eyes flick across the store and spot someone who looks like Carlos, wearing one of my old dresses with sunglasses that cover most of his face, suspiciously roaming the beauty aisle.

What the—what? My gaze dances around to see if I know anyone else. And there are my parents at the back of the line on checkout five, waiting to be served by Helga and the new girl. Their backs are to me, but I know it's them from the red handbag I got Mom for Christmas and Dad's balding head.

"What is going on?" I mumble.

My heart gallops wildly as my mind conjures up all the reasons my closest loved ones might be at my work at the same time. I remind myself to stay focused and direct my gaze to the next customer. A gentleman stands in front of me whose face is tilted toward the floor, the black baseball cap on his head makes it impossible to see his face. But a familiar scent of cologne whirls around me, sweeping me away like a tidal wave. He clears his throat, snapping me out of my head spin.

"Oh, sorry, sir," I say, pressing the conveyor belt button. A giant bouquet of flowers glides toward me. The closer the flowers get to me, the quicker my pulse races. My hands tremble as I realize I'm in the presence of Sean. I find the courage to slowly look up at him, and I'm met by his easy grin and hopeful eyes. All the breath whooshes out of me.

"Sean?"

He grins even wider and indicates the flowers with his chin. "Just those today, thanks."

I throw him a look of suspicion and pick the flowers up to scan them through. "For me?" I joke sassily. He winks, pulling his wallet from his pocket.

"Oh, are you going to pay for them today!" I marvel.

The corner of his mouth curls, and his gaze turns from gentle to piercing.

"Will that be all today, sir?"

He extends his palm. "Wait," he pulls a small box from his pocket. "Just one more thing." He gently places the box on the conveyor belt.

My starry eyes are glued to the box like it's a potential bomb. I swallow hard before pressing the conveyor belt button. I feel curious eyes on me. The store grows so quiet you can hear Helga let out a discrete fart.

Seconds away from receiving the box, the conveyor belt stops, making a churning noise. I gasp impatiently. Small exclamations and murmurs trickle around the store. Aggressively, I bang on the button while maintaining an affectionate gaze with Sean. But to my dismay, it won't budge.

"Let me," Sean says in his deep honey-laced voice. He sweeps the box up, which now looks even tinier in his big hand, and holds it before me. With a big smile, he opens it. I almost choke at the sight of a white-gold eighteen carat princess-cut diamond ring. Loud gasps ripple through the store as I cover my mouth with my hands and attempt to keep myself together.

"I'm sorry I made you pretend to be someone you're not. Because the only person I want to be with is you."

A dramatic gasp behind me makes me turn around to see Madeline, hands to her chest. Clifford stands next to her and gives me a comforting nod. When I turn around to face Sean, his knee is on the floor. I peer over the counter and hear the words.

"Sal, will you marry me?"

When I'm sure my voice won't crack, I gently speak. "Me?"

"Uh, yep. You Sal."

I hear a cry of happiness from Mom while Dad gives me a big thumbs up. Carlos, Fran, and Piper join them in a cute little huddle cheering me on with bright brimming eyes.

A long moment of silence filled with anticipation engulfs the whole store. Then I look into Sean's eyes and extend my hand. "Yes, Sean Maxwell, I will marry you."

An uproar of cheerful noise bubbles around the store. Sean stands up and places the ring on my shaky finger, laughing joyfully. He leans over, grabs me by my waist and places me on the conveyor belt.

"I love you, Sal."

If my face were a painting, it would be full of sunshine, rainbows, sparkles, and heart emojis. I throw my arms around his neck and kiss him. The kiss is soft, gentle, understated. Just how I like it, especially while so many eyes are upon us. Then I think, *to hell with it!* I pull him in closer, not caring what anyone thinks and kiss him as if I've never kissed him before.

The eruption of whistles, cheers and joyous banter makes me gently pull away. I bashfully look at him before resting my head on his shoulder. Helga approaches us.

"Congratulations, Sally. It looks like you've had a winning week." Helga combs her squinty eyes over Sean. "I've seen you before."

I smile at Sean and then back at Helga. "Hey, aren't you that runaway food grabber Sal put in jail?" Helga asks.

Sean's smirk grows into a laugh. "That would be me, I'm afraid."

Confusion crosses Helga's face. "Gee, you sure know how to choose 'em, Sal."

I smile at her before I look at the clock.

"Go on, get out of here already."

"Really, Helga?"

"Unless you want to stay behind and close?"

I shake my head, smiling. I glance up at Sean, he swoops me up and carries me in his arms. "Come on, let's get you out of here."

We make for the exit through a roaring, clapping crowd. "Sean, wait!"

Sean stops and looks down at me.

"We haven't paid for the flowers."

He chuckles and reverses his steps to where Helga stands with folded arms. "It's on us this time, Sal. Good luck out there, kiddo."

The excited crowd watches us leave. Lenny opens the door for us, and I call goodbye to him. Then we're greeted by an enormous handmade *Congratulations!* sign that Derek, Victoria and Katie hold with kind smiles. I gasp and wave at them before turning to Sean. "Is this for real?"

"Does this feel real to you?"

He leans into me, and I lose myself in his kiss.

The End

Epilogue

Four weeks later

"HONEY, I'M HOME!" I sing, skipping through Sean's—*our*—living room.

"How was your day, babe?" Sean asks, kissing me.

"Amazing! Being on set makes me feel alive again. How was yours?"

"Well ..." he draws out a long pause. "*Nevada Wildlife Magazine* got back to me."

"And?" I ask, wrapping my hands around my face in excitement.

"They're using my photographs, and they offered me a job!"

I scream, throwing my arms around him.

"The pay's not much. But it's a foot in the door."

"I knew you would do it!"

He chuckles. "I know you did. Why do you think I'm marrying you?" He winks at me as he walks to the leather couch where Oscar sleeps. "On another note, I spoke to Brady today."

"Please don't say he wants Piper's number again?" I demand, narrowing my eyes.

He gives me a look that confirms I'm right.

"He'll have to wait in line because every man wants her number. Besides, she has a boyfriend!"

"That's what I told him. But he's persistent."

He wraps one arm around me, smirking. "So, I was thinking. Now that I'm going to be employed—if a winter wedding is what you want—let's do it!"

I explode with excitement and pour my whole body onto his. He laughs and settles into a warm embrace with me. "On one condition."

I wiggle an eyebrow, and his eyes land on the cushions Oscar is nestled among.

"You get rid of those fluffy pink things."

I smile, aware it had only been a matter of time before he plucked up the courage to ask. Plus, the pink does *not* agree with his decor. Let's just say I'm quickly learning that relationships are all about compromise. He even makes vegetarian sausages when I know he wants steak. Now *that's* love.

"Oh, and can you please rinse your dishes before putting them in the dishwasher?"

I pout and blush. "Deal!"

A Love Note

Thank you so much for reading *Single Sal!* I hope this story made you laugh and swoon and ultimately reflect on how amazing you are just being *you* (the way you are).

I loved writing this story, and I can't wait to share more about the lives of Sal, Piper and Fran with you all. To be the first to know about future novels and blog posts about dating and love, please visit emmylove.com.

If you enjoyed *Single Sal*, feel free to leave an honest review. Reviews are like a mom's warm hug to an author—always appreciated.

Until we meet again,
Love, laugh and dream.

Emmy xx

Acknowledgments

I cannot express enough gratitude to my talented pre-publishing team, who took the time to help make this story what it is today.

Thank you to my beta readers—Ryan Walker, Nicole Ugwueze, Lenore Moreau, and Kerri Coveney.

To my editor, Bonnie Stevenson, your eagle eyes and exceptional talent gave me the confidence to finally publish.

To my illustrator and designer, Rebecca Rhodes, thank you for being such a talented rockstar who brought my vision to life.

Finally, to my loving, supportive family, who let me be who I am without judgement. You never doubted me, even when I doubted myself. Because of you, I keep writing.

About Author

Emmy Love is a New Zealander, with a background in digital marketing, acting and storytelling.

Her debut novel *Single Sal* was inspired by her own single status and journey of self-discovery, including learning to accept herself—flaws and all!

Los Angeles, where the story is set, is one of Emmy's favorite cities, and she dreams of returning someday.

When she's not busy writing romantic comedies, you can find her entertaining her dogs, reading, geeking out on sci-fi movies, and swooning over her crush Henry Cavill.

You can stay connected with Emmy on the following socials, where she shares all kinds of bookish and behind-the-scenes stuff. (And maybe a few pics of her dogs.)

- instagram.com/emmyloveauthor/
- facebook@emmylove
- tiktok.com/@emmyloveauthor